W9-BAC-439

Meoud reached for the bottle. "Join me," he invited. "A man should never drink alone, not when he is haunted by specters of the past. I was the second highest in my class," he mourned. "Everyone predicted a brilliant future for me in the guild. It seemed I could do no wrong. So tell me, friend, what am I doing on this isolated world?"

"Brooding," said Dumarest, "dreaming of what might have been, obsessed with past opportunities and past mistakes, looking back instead of forward. You surprise me—a man of business to be so sentimental! How many of your guild suffer from such weakness?"

"How many travelers chase a legend?" Meoud was sharp. "I have heard the stories, my friend. I know why you chose to live in Lowtown instead of taking a cubicle here in the station, of your searching and questioning. *Earth*," he said. "How can a world have such a name? It has no meaning. All planets are made of earth. Why not then call Scar dirt, or soil, or loam, or even ground? It would make as much sense."

Dumarest looked down at his hand where it clenched around the glass. "Earth is no legend," he said flatly. "The planet is real and, one day, *I shall find it*."

THE JESTER AT SCAR

The Dumarest of Terra Series by E.C. Tubb, from *Ace Science Fiction:*

THE JESTER AT SCAR

E.C. TUBB

SF

ace books

A Division of Charter Communications Inc.
A GROSSET & DUNLAP COMPANY
51 Madison Avenue
New York, New York 10010

THE JESTER AT SCAR
Copyright © 1970 by E.C. Tubb

DEDICATION:
To Hilda

An ACE Book

This Ace printing: August 1982
Published simultaneously in Canada

2 4 6 8 0 9 7 5 3 1
Manufactured in the United States of America

THE JESTER AT SCAR

Chapter One

In the lamplight, the woman's face was drawn, anxious. "Earl," she said. "Earl, please wake up."

Dumarest opened his eyes, immediately alert. "What is it?"

"Men," she said, "moving outside. I thought I heard noises from the street, screams and the sound of laughter." The guttering flame of the lamp threw patches of moving shadow across her face as she straightened from the side of the bed. "Cruel laughter, it had an ugly sound."

He frowned, listening and hearing nothing but the normal violence of the night. "A dream," he suggested. "A trick of the wind."

"No." She was emphatic. "I've lived on this world too long to be mistaken. I heard something unnatural, the noise of men searching, perhaps. But it was there; I didn't imagine it."

Dumarest threw back the covers and rose, the soft lamp light shining on his hard, white skin and accentuating the thin scars of old wounds. The interior of the hut was reeking with damp, the ground soggy beneath his bare feet. He took his clothes from the couch and quickly dressed in pants, knee-high boots and a sleeved tunic which fell to mid-thigh. Carefully he fastened the high collar around his throat. From beneath the pillow he took a knife and sheathed it in his right boot.

"Listen" said the woman urgently. The lamp was a bowl of translucent plastic containing oil and a floating wick. It shook a little in her hand. "Listen!"

He tensed, ears straining against the ceaseless drum of rain, the gusting sough of wind. The wind slackened a little then blew with redoubled force, sending a fine spray of rain through the poorly constructed walls of the shack. More rain came through the sloping, unguttered roof and thin streams puddled the floor. Among such a medley of sounds it would be easy to imagine voices.

Relaxing, Dumarest glanced at the woman. She stood tall, the lamp now steady in her hand. Her eyes were set wide apart, deep beneath their brows; thick, brown hair had been cropped close to her rounded skull. Her hands were slim and delicate, but her figure was concealed by the motley collection of clothing she wore for warmth and protection. Beyond her a few embers glowed in an open fireplace built of stone. Dumarest crossed to it, dropped to his knees beside a box and fed scraps of fuel from the box to the embers. Flames rose, flickered and illuminated the woman's home.

It wasn't much. The bed where he'd slept was in one corner of the single room which was about ten feet by twelve. A curtain, now drawn back, split the single room in half during times of rest. The woman's couch rested in the far corner beyond the curtain. A table, benches and chests, all of rough construction, completed the furnishings. The walls were of stones bedded in dirt; uprights supported the sagging roof. Against the dirt and stone, fragments of brightly colored plastic-sheeting merged with salvaged wrappings from discarded containers.

Smoke wafted from the burning fuel and made him cough.

"Quiet!" warned the woman. She turned to Dumarest. "They're coming back," she said. "I can hear them."

He rose, listened and heard the squelch of approaching footsteps.

They halted, and something hard slammed against the barred door.

"Open!" The voice was flat and harsh. "We are travelers in need of shelter; open before we drown."

Lamplight glittered from her eyes. "Earl?"

"A moment." Dumarest stepped quietly forward and stood beside the door. It would open inward and away from where he stood, giving him a clear field if action should be necessary. His hand dipped to his boot and rose bearing nine inches of razor-sharp steel. "Don't argue with them," he said softly. "Just open the door and step back a little. Don't look towards me. Hold the lamp above your head."

She glanced at the knife held sword-fashion in his hand. "And you?"

"That depends." His face was expressionless. "If they are genuine travelers seeking accommodation, send them on their way; or take them in if you prefer their company to mine. If they are besotted fools looking for something to entertain them, they will leave when they discover there is nothing for them here. If not . . ." He shrugged. "Open the door."

Wind gusted as she swung open the panel, driving in a spray of rain and the ubiquitous smell of the planet. From outside grated a voice, harsh against the wind.

"Hold, Brephor. No need to knock again. You there, woman, your name is Selene?"

"It is."

"And you sell food and shelter. That, at least, was what we were told." The voice became impatient. "Step forward and show yourself; I have no wish to talk to shadows."

Silently she obeyed, moving the lamp so as to let the guttering light shine on her face; she remained impassive at the sound of sharply indrawn breath.

"Acid," she said evenly. "I was contaminated with parasitical spores on the face and neck; there was no time to consider my beauty. It was a matter of burning them away or watching me die. Sometimes I think they made the wrong dicision." The lamp trembled a little as she fought old memories. "But I forget myself, gentlemen. You are in need. What is your pleasure?"

"With you? Nothing." Boots squelched in mud as the speaker turned from the doorway. "Come, Brephor. We waste our time."

"A moment, Hendris. You decide too fast." The second voice was indolent, purring with the sadistic anticipation of a hunting feline. "The woman has a scarred face, true, but is it essential that a man look at her face? Such a disfigurement, to some, could even be attractive. I am sure that you follow my thought, Hendris. If the face is bad, the rest of her could be most—interesting."

Hendris was sharp. "You scent something, Brephor?"

"Perhaps." His indolence sharpened into something ugly. The purr became a snarl as Brephor loomed in the doorway. "Tell me woman, how do you live?"

"I sell food and shelter," she said flatly. "And the monks are kind."

"The monks? Those beggars of the Church of Universal Brotherhood?" His laugh was a sneer. "They feed you?"

"They give what they can."

"And that is enough? No," he mused answering himself. "It cannot be enough; the monks do not give all to one and nothing to another. You need food and oil, fuel and clothing, medicines too, perhaps. In order to survive you need more than the monks can provide." He extended his hand; the back was covered with a fine down. Steel had been wedded to the fingernails; the metal was razor-edged and needle-pointed. The tips pricked her skin. "Speak truthfully, woman, or I will close my hand and tear out your throat. You need lodgers in order to survive; is that not so?"

She swallowed, not answering. Spots of blood shone like tiny rubies at the points of steel.

"We will assume that it is so," purred Brephor from where he stood in darkness. "And yet when we, two travelers, come seeking food and shelter, we are repulsed. You did not invite us in out of the rain; you did not suggest terms; you were not even curious as to how we knew both your name and business. But that is acceptable. You are dependent on publicity and offer a commission to those who send you clients." The spots of blood grew, swelling to break and fall in widening streams from the lacerating claws. "I scent a mystery, woman. You are in business, but have no time for customers. Perhaps you no longer need to sell food and shelter. It could be that you have someone now to provide, someone lurking in the darkness." The purr hardened and became vicious. "Tell me, woman!"

"Tell him," said Dumarest as he stepped from where he stood against the wall. The reaction was immediate. Brephor straightened his arm with a jerk, sending the woman staggering backwards, the lamp flickering as she fought to retain her balance. As she stumbled he sprang through the doorway, landed and turned to face Dumarest.

"So," he purred. "Our friend who lurks in shadows. The brave man who stands and watches as his woman is molested. Tell me, coward, what is your name?"

Silently Dumarest studied the intruder. His eyes were huge beneath lowering brows, ears slightly pointed, mouth pursed over prominent canines. His face and neck were covered with the same fine down as the backs of his hands. Brephor was a cat-man, a mutated sport from some lonely world, the genes of his forebears jumbled by radiation. He would be fast and vicious, a stranger to the concept of mercy, a stranger also to the concept of obedience.

"I asked you a question, coward," he said. "What is your name!"

"Dumarest," said Earl, "a traveler like yourself." He lifted his left hand so as to draw attention away from his right and the knife held tight against his leg. The ring he wore caught the light, the flat, red stone glowing like a pool of freshly spilled blood. Brephor looked at it and flared his nostrils.

Abruptly he attacked.

Metal flashed as he raked his claws at Dumarest's eyes. At the same time his free hand reached out to trap the knife and his knee jerked up and forward in a vicious blow at the groin. Dumarest swayed backwards, twisting and lifting his knife beyond reach. He felt something touch his cheek, falling to tear at his tunic and becoming a furred and sinewy wrist as he caught it with his left hand. The stabbing knee thudded against his thigh and, for a moment, Brephor was off balance.

Immediately Dumarest swung up the knife and thrust along the line of the arm, driving the blade deep into the cat-man's neck just below the ear; he twisted it so as to free the steel. The force of the impact sent them both towards the door. Dumarest regained his balance, jerked free the knife and sent the dead man toppling from the hut.

A face showed as a pale blob against the darkness, lit by the small flame of the lamp within the hut. Something bright rose as the woman screamed a warning.

"Earl! He's got a gun!"

Fire spat from the muzzle of the weapon as Dumarest threw the knife. He saw the face fall away, the hilt sprouting from one eye and a ribbon of blood running down the ruff of beard. The blood was immediately washed away by the rain.

"Be careful!" Selene lifted the lamp, sheltering the flame. "There could be others."

He ignored her, springing from the doorway to recover the knife. Rain hammered at his unprotected head, slammed against the shoulders of his tunic and sent little spurts of mud leaping up from the semi-liquid ooze. In seconds it had washed the blade clean. Dumarest sheathed it and looked to either side; he saw nothing but darkness relieved only by the weak glimmers of light coming from behind scraps of transparent plastic or through cracks in disintegrating walls.

"Earl—"

"Give me the lamp," he snapped, "quickly!"

The flame danced as he held it close to the faces of the dead men. Hendris had none of the characteristics of his companion, but that meant little. They could have come from different worlds. If they had grown up together it still meant nothing. If Brephor was the norm, then Hendris could have been an atavist; if Hendris was the norm, Brephor would have been a freak. Both, to Dumarest, were strangers.

He found the gun and examined it. It was a simple slug-thrower of cheap manufacture and used an explosive to drive the solid projectile. Dumarest threw it into the darkness. It was useless without matching ammunition and a laser was far more efficient. Handing the lamp back to Selene, he dragged both men into the shelter of the hut. Straightening, he looked at the woman.

"If you want anything, take it," he said. "But don't waste time doing it."

She hesitated.

"Strip them," he said curtly. "Are you so rich you can afford to throw away things of value?"

"You know I'm not, Earl," she protested. "But

if I take things which may later be recognized by a friend, I shall be blamed for having caused their deaths."

"Men like these have no friends," he said flatly. "Let's see what they were carrying."

The clothes were ordinary, but of a better quality than they seemed. There was money, a phial of drugs from Brephor, spare clips of ammunition for the discarded gun of the bearded man, and five rings of varying quality and size, all with red stones. Also there were a couple of sleeve knives and an igniter and flashlight with a self-charging cell, but nothing more of interest or value.

Dumarest frowned as he examined the rings. "Odd," he mused. "Why should they want to collect rings?"

"They were robbers," said the woman, "raiders. They saw your ring and thought to take it."

Slowly Dumarest shook his head.

"They were spoiling for trouble," she insisted. "The cat-man must have sensed your presence. He was a killer desiring sport." Her finger touched the phial of drugs. "Doped," she said. "Riding high, and fast! When he went for your eyes his hand was a blur. If you hadn't been even faster he would have torn out your eyes."

That was true enough. Dumarest opened the phial and cautiously tasted the contents. A euphoric, he guessed, probably wedded to slow-time so that the effect of the drug would be enhanced by the actual speeding up of the metabolism. If so, Brephor's speed was understandable; time, to him, had slowed so that he could do more in a second than could a normal man.

Dumarest sealed the phial and threw it on the

table. "Why?" he demanded. "Why should they have come here as they did? They weren't looking for shelter; they had enough money to buy that at the station. And they knew you had someone staying at your home."

"Coincidence," she said. "They were looking for sport and changed their minds when they saw my face."

"They were looking for something," he agreed. "The cat-man attacked as soon as he saw my ring." He looked at it, a warm patch against his finger, and idly ran his thumb over the stone. "They had five rings," he mused. "all with red stones. Did five men die to supply them?"

"They were raiders" she insisted stubbornly, "men who hoped to rob and kill in the cover of the night."

"Yes," said Dumarest. "You are probably correct." He looked at the pile of clothing and the small heap of the dead men's possessions. "Take it." he said, "all of it."

Her eyes fell to where the two bodies lay sprawled on the floor. "And those?"

"Leave them to me."

The huts were built on the slope of a valley, the only feasible place on a planet where the rain fell with the relentless force it did on Scar. All through the thirty-day winter the skies emptied their burden of water, the rain washing away the soil, garbage and refuse, carrying it down to the valley which was now a small sea of ooze.

Dumarest picked up the cat-man; his muscles bulged beneath his tunic as he˙ supported the weight. Cautiously, he walked through the cluster of shacks to where the ground fell abruptly away from beneath his feet. He heaved, waited, and turned when he heard the splash of the body. The bearded man followed, sinking into the morass, food for the parasitical fungi, the bacteria and the anaerobic spores.

Slowly Dumarest walked back to the hut. The door was open, the guttering flame of the lamp illuminating the interior and casting a patch of brightness on the mud outside. He paused at the opening; the dead men's effects had vanished from sight. Selene looked at him from where she stood beside the table.

"You're leaving," she said, "going to the station, back to the field."

Dumarest nodded. "You don't need me," he said, "not now, and it's almost spring. I would have been leaving in any case."

Her hand rose and touched the scar on the side of her face, the seared and puckered blotch which ran over cheek and neck. "You don't have to go, Earl. You know that."

"I know it."

"Then—"

"Goodbye, Selene."

He was three steps away from the hut when she slammed the door.

The rain eased a little as he climbed the slope towards the landing field where the only really permanent buildings on the planet were clustered. Here were the warehouses, the stores, the factor's post, processing plant, commissary and the raised and sheltered dwellings of Hightown. They were empty now. Tourists came only at the beginning of summer, but others resided all the year round.

One of the buildings, built solidly of fused stone
and with a transparent roof which could be dark-
ened during the time of sun and heat, shone like a
lambent pearl in the darkness. Underfoot the yielding mud gave way to a solid surface and Dumarest
lengthened his stride. Light shone on a trough of
running water and he stepped into it, washing the
slime from his boots before reaching for the door.
Hot air blasted as he stepped into the vestibule; the
air was replaced by a spray of sterilizing compounds as he shut the door. Three seconds later the
spray ceased and the inner door swung open.

"Earl!" A man lifted his hand in greeting as
Dumarest stepped from the vestibule. He sat at a
table littered with cards, dice, chips and a marked
cloth. Three hemispheres of plastic about an inch
wide stood ranked before him on the table. "Care
to play?"

"Later," said Dumarest.

"Well, come and test my skill." The gambler was
a jovial man with a round paunch and thick, decep-
tively agile fingers. Busily he moved the three hemispheres. Under one he slipped a small ball, moved
them all and looked questioningly at Dumarest.
"Well? Where is it?"

Dumarest reached out and touched one of the
shells.

"Wrong! Try again."

"Later, Ewan."

"You'll come back?"

Dumarest nodded and moved across the room.
Tables and chairs littered the floor. An open bar
stood against one wall, a closed canteen against another. The remaining space was filled with counters
fashioned for display. Men sat or sprawled and

talked in low whispers or moved languidly about. Del Meoud, the local factor, sat at a table and brooded over his glass. He wore the bright colors of his guild, which gave him a spurious appearance of youth; but his face was etched with deep lines beneath the stylized pattern of his beard.

His eyes flickered as Dumarest approached him.

"Join me," he invited. Then, as Dumarest took the proffered chair he said, "I warned you: do a woman a favor and she will reward you with anger. Your face," he explained. "You were lucky that she did not get an eye."

Dumarest touched his cheek and looked at the blood on his fingers. He remembered the razor-edged steel Brephor had flung at his eyes. Looking down he saw scratches in the gray plastic of his tunic. They were deep enough to reveal the gleam of protective mesh buried in the material. He dabbed again at his cheek.

"Let it bleed," advised the factor. "Who knows what hell-spore may have settled on the wound?"

"In winter?"

"Winter, spring, summer—Scar lives up to its name." Meoud reached for his bottle. "Join me," he invited. "A man should never drink alone, not when he is haunted by specters of the past." He filled a second glass and pushed it towards his guest. "I was the second highest in my class," he mourned. "Everyone predicted a brilliant future for me in the guild. It seemed that I could do no wrong. So tell me, friend, what am I doing on this isolated world?"

"Growing old," said Dumarest drily. "You had too much luck, all of it bad."

Meoud drank, refilled his glass and drank again.

"No," he said bitterly, "not bad luck, a bad woman—a girl with hair of shimmering gold and skin of sun-kissed velvet, slim, lithe, a thing of sun and summer—she danced on my heart and brought nothing but sorrow."

Dumarest sipped his wine. It had the harsh, arid taste of the local production and still contained the drifting motes of unfiltered spores.

"She gave me a modicum of pleasure," continued the factor, "but I paid for it with a mountain of pain. A high price, my friend, but I was young and proud, and ambition rode me like a man rides an animal." The bottle made small crystalline noises as he helped himself to more wine. "Was it so wrong to be ambitious? Without it, what is life? We are not beasts to be born and breed and wait for death. Always we must reach a little higher, strive to obtain a little more, travel a little faster. The philosophy of living, ambition!"

He drank and set down the empty glass. Reaching for the bottle he found it empty and irritably ordered another. He poured the glasses full as the barman walked away.

"Her father was the Manager of Marque," he said. "True, she was but his seventeenth daughter, yet she was still of the ruling house. I thought my fortune assured when I contracted for her hand—the influence, the high associations! The guild is kind to those who have influence in high places, kinder still to those with connections with rulers. I tell you, my friend, for a time I walked on golden clouds." Meoud drank. "It was a dream," he said bitterly. "All I had accomplished was to engineer my own ruin."

Dumarest thought he understood. "She left you?"

"She made me bankrupt," corrected the factor. "On Marque a husband is responsible for the debts of his wife. The guild saved me from bondage, but I ended with nothing; no wife, no position, nothing but a limited charity. And so I wait on Scar."

"Brooding," said Dumarest, "dreaming of what might have been, obsessed with past opportunities and past mistakes, looking back instead of forward. You surprise me—a man of business to be so sentimental! How many of your guild suffer from such weakness?"

"How many travelers chase a legend?" Meoud was sharp. He had drunk too deeply and confessed too much, but the winter dragged and the future was bleak. "I have heard the stories, my friend. I know why you chose to live in Lowtown instead of taking a cubicle here at the station, of your searching and questioning. Earth," he said. "How can a world have such a name? It has no meaning. All planets are made of earth. Why not then call Scar dirt, or soil, or loam, or even ground? It would make as much sense."

Dumarest looked down at his hand where it was clenched around the glass. "Earth is no legend," he said flatly. "The planet is real and, one day, I shall find it."

"A legend." Meoud poured them both more wine. "Is that what brought you to Scar?"

"I was on Crane," said Dumarest. "Before that on Zagazin, on Toom, on Hope,"—he looked at his ring—"on Solis and before that . . ." He shrugged. "Does it matter? The ship which carried me here was the first to leave when I sought passage on Crane."

Meoud frowned. "And you took it? Just like that?"

"Why not? It was heading in the right direction, out, away from the center. The stars are thin as seen from Earth."

"As they are from many lonely worlds," pointed out the factor.

"True," admitted Dumarest. "But it was a world with a blue sky by day and a silver moon by night; the stars made patterns which wheeled across the sky. I shall recognize them when I see them again. In the meantime, if you should hear anyone speak of Earth, you will let me know?"

Meoud nodded, staring into his glass. *I should tell him,* he thought, *convince him that he is chasing an illusion, a dream world fabricated when he was a child as a region in which to escape harsh reality. But who am I to rob a man of his dream, his dream and his reason for existence?*

He lifted his glass and drank, knowing that some things are best left unsaid.

Dumarest left the factor to the consolation of his wine. The buildings of the station were dreary with winter inactivity, the residents those who had to stay from reasons of investment or duty. Others, whom the vagaries of space travel had brought early to the planet, rested in deep sleep until the summer. Still more huddled miserably in their damp quarters in Lowtown; the travelers whom chance had stranded on a non-productive world, the desperate who lacked the cost of a low passage to some other planet.

Ewan looked up as Dumarest passed his table.

"Earl," he said, "please watch. I need the practice."

"You're skillful enough," said Dumarest. "You don't need my opinion."

"I do," insisted the gambler. "I want to try

something new. These shells," he explained. "As I move them about I slip this little ball beneath one. I can manipulate it as I wish." His pudgy hands moved the shells with deft skill. "Right. Now pick out the shell with the ball. Guess correctly and I will give you five. Guess wrongly and you pay me the same. Deal?"

"The odds are in your favor," pointed out Dumarest. "Two to one."

Ewan shrugged. "The house has to have some edge. Now pick."

Dumarest smiled and rested the tip of a finger on one of the shells. It was the finger on which he wore his ring. With his free hand he tipped the remaining two shells over. Neither hid the little ball.

"This one," he said, tapping the remaining hemisphere. "Pay me."

Ewan scowled. "You cheated. That isn't the right way to play."

"It's my way," said Dumarest, "and others will do the same. You've had a cheap lesson; take my advice and stick to cards and dice. It will be safer."

Ewan handed over the money. "Not if you're with me, Earl," he said. "How about it? A fifth of the profit if you will act as bodyguard and shill."

Dumarest shook his head.

"A quarter then? I can't make it more. I've got to pay for the concession, hold capital for the next season and hold more for emergencies. A quarter, Earl, just for standing by in case of trouble and leading the betting. You could do it in your sleep. Certain cash, Earl, a high passage at least; you can't lose."

The gambler frowned as Dumarest showed no interest.

"What's the alternative?" he demanded. "Acting

as guide to some fat tourist, risking your life hunting rare spores, collecting fungi for the processing sheds?" Ewan blew out his cheeks and shook his head. "You should know better; there are easier ways to make money. You're fast, quick as any man I've seen. You've got a look about you which would make any trouble-maker think twice. A third, Earl. That's as high as I can go. A clear third of the profit. What do you say?"

"Thank you," said Dumarest, "but no."

"A gambling layout is a good place to pick up gossip," said Ewan shrewdly. "Most of the new arrivals want to test their luck and they talk while doing it." He picked up a deck of cards and riffled them, his pudgy fingers almost covering the slips of plastic. "Sure you won't change your mind?"

"If I do I'll let you know," said Dumarest. He hesitated, looking down at the gambler. Had Ewan been trying to tell him something? He resisted the impulse to find out. Two men were dead and the less said about either of them the better.

He crossed to where a layout of colored holograms showed a variety of fungi in all stages of growth in perfect, three-dimensional representation. Each was labeled. The display was the property of a company operating the processing sheds and the fungi were the strains they wanted.

"Simple, safe and secure," said an ironic voice at his side. "All you have to do, Earl, is to turn yourself into a mobile hopper. Go out and drag back a few tons of fungi and, with luck, you'll get enough profit to keep you in food for a week."

"You don't have to do it," said Dumarest evenly. "No one is holding a knife to your throat."

Heldar coughed, holding his hand before his

mouth as he fought for air. "Damn spores," he muttered at last. "One in the lungs is one too many." He scowled at the display. "You don't know," he said bitterly. "When hunger has you by the guts you don't stop to think of what the small print says. You just want a square meal."

"And you got it," said Dumarest. "So why are you complaining?"

Heldar scowled. "It's all right for you," he said. "You've got money. You can—"

He broke off, looking upwards. Dumarest followed his example. Every man in the place stopped what he was doing and stared at the roof.

The silence was almost tangible.

For weeks they had been deafened by the unremitting thunder of winter rain.

Chapter Two

The captain was effusive with his apologies. "My lord," he said, bowing, "my lady, I regret to inform you that we are no longer on schedule."

Jocelyn raised his eyebrows. "Regret?"

His wife was more to the point. "Why?" she demanded. "How can it be that we are as you say? Are you no longer capable of plotting a simple course from star to star?"

The captain bowed even more deeply. As master of the sole vessel owned by the ruler of Jest, his position was an enviable one; and if at times he wished that his command had been a little more modern, he kept such thoughts to himself.

"We became embroiled in the fringe of an interstellar storm, my lady," he explained. "The magnetic flux disturbed our instruments and retarded our passage a matter of some three days. I can, of course, accelerate our speed if you so desire."

As you could have done in the first place, thought Jocelyn. *So why report the matter at all? Fear,* he decided. *To safeguard himself against the report of a spy, to insure himself against the ambition of a junior officer.* He felt his lips twist into a familiar wryness.

Did he really appear so formidable?

"My lord?" The captain was sweating. "My lady?"

"You shall be flogged," snapped Adrienne, "stripped of your command! I shall—"

"Do nothing without due consideration," interrupted Jocelyn curtly. "The man is hardly to blame for the elements, and on Jest, we do not use the barbaric means of punishment common on other worlds."

"Barbaric!" He had touched her. Spots of color glowed on her thin cheeks, the anger reflecting itself in her narrowed eyes. "Are you referring to Eldfane?"

"Did I mention your home world?" Jocelyn smiled into her eyes. "You are too sensitive, my dear, too quick to take offense. But the fault is not yours. Those who trained you when young are to blame; they discouraged your childish laughter. That was wrong. In this universe, my darling wife, laughter is the only answer a man can make to his destiny, the only challenge he can throw into the faces of his gods."

"Superstition!" Contempt replaced her anger. "My father warned me of your peculiar ways. That is why—" She broke off, conscious of the listening captain. "Why do you linger?"

"My lady." His bow was mechanical, an automatic response rooted in defense. "My lord," he said straightening, "I await your instructions."

"Have they changed?" Jocelyn frowned. "Are we not proceeding to Jest?"

"We were, my lord, but the storm has placed us in a peculiar relationship. We are equidistant from both Jest and Scar and our relative speed is common to both. That means we can reach either in the same amount of time." The captain took a deep breath. "I am not a superstitious man, my lord, but the workings of destiny can sometimes reveal itself in strange forms."

"Such as a storm, a malfunction of the instruments and a peculiar coincidence?" Jocelyn nodded thoughtfully. "You could be right, Captain. You think we should proceed to Scar?"

The captain bowed, disclaiming responsibility. "The decision is yours, my lord."

And the derision should the journey be pointless, thought Jocelyn ironically. But could any journey ever be that? Jest waited with the same eternal problems and could wait a little longer without coming to harm. It would almost be a kindness to delay their arrival. Adrienne was accustomed to a softer world and less independence. She would have troubles enough once they had landed and she had been installed as his queen.

He glanced at her, noting the thin arrogance of her profile, the imperious tilt of her head. Strange how those with the least reason adopted the greater dignity, stranger still how the bare facts could be transmuted by pompous phraseology. He, the ruler of Jest, had married the daughter of Elgone, the Elder of Eldfane. If the people thought of it as a love-match, they were more stupid than he guessed. As a dowry she had brought him one hundred thousand tons of basic staples, the revenues from her estate on Eldfane, a million units of trading credit to be used on her home world, the services of an engineering corps for three years; and the promise of an obsolete space vessel when one should be available.

The promise meant nothing. The staples were already on their way, sealed in freight cans flung into space by tractors, aimed so as to orbit Jest until they could be collected by this very ship. The revenues would dwindle, the credit likewise as inflation and profiteering greed slashed their value. The engineering corps would turn out to be a handful of advisers strong on suggestion but woefully lacking in application.

All he would have left would be a shrewish woman to sit on his double throne.

All?

He felt his lips twist in their familiar expression, the wry grin he had developed when a boy and which was his defense against hurt, pain and hopeless despair. *To smile, to treat everything as a joke— how else to remain sane?*

"My dear," he said to Adrienne. "We are faced with the need to make a decision, to go on to Jest or to head for Scar. It is a problem which can be solved in many ways. We could spin a coin; we could arrange a number of random selective-choices, such as the first officer to walk through that door would decide for us by his first word; or we could apply logic and knowledge to guide our choice."

The edges of her thin nostrils turned white as she controlled her anger. "Is this a time for foolish jesting?"

He smiled blandly. "Can a jest ever be foolish?"

"On Eldfane," she said tightly, "we have a means of discouraging those who hold similar beliefs. Life is serious and no cause for mirth."

"And you make it so by the use of whips, acid and fire," said Jocelyn. "But, on Eldfane, laughter has an ugly sound." He shook his head, abruptly weary of the pointless exchange. As long as the woman kept her part of the marriage contract he would be content: food, credit, the help of trained and educated men, and, above all, a son.

He glanced at the captain as the man cleared his throat. "What is it?"

"If I may make a suggestion, my lord?"

Jocelyn nodded.

"The problem could be resolved by one trained in such matters. The cyber would doubtless be happy to advise."

Jocelyn frowned. He had forgotten Yeon, the final part of Adrienne's dowry, added almost as an afterthought by Elgone, which he had reluctantly accepted. He had been reluctant because he had an instinctive mistrust of a man who could not laugh.

"Thank you, Captain," said Adrienne before Jocelyn could speak. "At last we have had a sensible suggestion. Be so good as to ask the cyber to attend us."

"No," said Jocelyn.

She turned and looked at him, fine eyebrows arched over contemptuous eyes. "Husband?"

"Never mind." He surrendered. "Do as Her Majesty commands." She was, after all, his wife.

Yeon came within minutes, a living flame in the rich scarlet of his robe, the seal of the Cyclan burning on his breast. He stood, facing Jocelyn, hands tucked within the wide sleeves of his gown.

"You sent for me, my lord?"

"I did." Jocelyn turned to where Adrienne sat in a chair covered in ancient leather. "Do you wish to state the problem?" He sighed as she shook her head. "Very well, I will do so."

The cyber stood silent when he had finished.

"Are you in doubt as to the answer?" Jocelyn felt a sudden satisfaction in the thought that he had beaten the man, presented him with a problem to which he could find no solution. The satisfaction died as Yeon met his eyes.

"My lord, I am in some doubt as to what you require of me."

"I thought it simple. Do we go to Jest or to Scar?"

"The decision is yours, my lord. All I can do is to advise you on the logical development of certain actions you may care to take. In this case I lack sufficient data to be able to extrapolate the natural sequence of events." His voice was a smooth modulation carefully trained so as to contain no irritating factors, a neutral voice belonging to a neutral man.

A neuter, rather, thought Jocelyn savagely. *A machine of flesh and blood devoid of all emotion and the capability of feeling. A man who could experience no other pleasure than that of mental acheivement. But clever. Give him a handful of facts and, from them, he would build more, enough for him to make uncannily accurate predictions as to the course of future events.*

Adrienne stirred in her chair. "Is there anything you can tell us about Scar?"

Yeon turned to face her. His shaven head gleamed in the lights as if of polished bone, the soft yellow of his skin accentuating the skull-like appearance of his face against the warmth of his cowl.

"Scar, my lady, is a small world with a peculiar ecology. The year is ninety days long and, as the planet has no rotation at all, the seasons are compressed between one dawn and another. There are thirty days for winter, during which it rains continuously and the same for summer, during which it gets very hot; the remainder is split between spring and autumn. The population is transient and consists mostly of tourists."

Jocelyn cleared his throat. "What else?"

"Exports, my lord?"

"That and anything else which may be of interest."

"The natural vegetation is fungoid, both saprophytes and parasites of various types and sizes. Traders call to purchase various spores which have some value in industry. There is also the aesthetic beauty of the planet, which holds strong appeal to artists."

"Spores," mused Jocelyn. He sat, thinking. "Have you yet assimilated the information you required on Jest?"

"Not yet, my lord."

"Then more time would not be a total waste." He reached for the bell to summon the captain. "We shall go to Scar."

"Are you sure?" Adrienne was ironic. "No spin of a coin, or casting of runes, perhaps? Surely you have not based your decision on sheer logic!"

"Sometimes, my dear," he said sweetly, "destiny requires no outward symbol." He looked at the captain as he entered the cabin. "We go to Scar," he ordered. "When should we arrive?"

"On Scar, my lord?" The captain pursed his lips. "Early spring. I could delay if you wish."

"No," said Jocelyn. "Spring is a good time to arrive anywhere."

Later, alone, he took a coin from his pocket and studied the sides. One bore the imprint of his father's head, the reverse the arms of Jest. With his thumbnail he drew a line across the rounded cheek.

"Destiny," he whispered, and spun the coin.

He smiled as he looked down at his father's face.

Del Meoud stepped out of his office and was immediately blinded by swirling curtains of ruby mist. Impatiently he lifted a hand and swept the infrared screen down over his eyes. At once his vision cleared, the shapes of men showing as radiant phantoms against a luminous haze.

"Sergi!" he called. "Sergi! Over here"

The engineer was big, thick across the shoulders with a neck like a bole of a tree. He wore stained pants, boots, open tunic and a wide-brimmed hat dripped water. The screen across his eyes gave him a peculiar robotical look. "Factor?"

"You're behind schedule," said Meoud. "The blowers around Hightown should be operating by now. Why aren't they?"

"Snags," said the engineer bitterly. "Always snags. The pile should have been on full operation by now. The blowers are fixed and ready to go as soon as I get the power, but do those electricians care? Wait, they tell me, no point in rushing things. Hurry now, before a double-check has been made, could result in arc and delay." He spat into the mud. "If you ask me, they're afraid of getting their hands dirty; I could do better with a gang from Lowtown."

Meoud stifled a sigh. It was always the same. Each spring he swore that it would never happen again, but always it did. Little things united to build up into worrying delays. One day time would slip past too fast and summer would find him unprepared. In that case, not even the charity of the guild would serve to protect him.

He turned as a man came stamping through the mist.

"Factor?"

"What is it, Langel?"

"I'm short of men. If you want the area sprayed as you said, I've got to have more help." Langel, like Sergi, was on the resident maintenance staff.

"You've got all I can give you," snapped Meoud. He glared at Sergi, forgetting the other couldn't see his eyes. "How about your men? You aren't using them, are you?"

"I need them to adjust the blowers. Anyway, you can't spray until they're working, not unless you want the stuff to go all to hell."

That was true. Meoud scowled as he reviewed the problem. The trouble with Scar was that everything had to be done in so much of a hurry once spring had arrived. The rains stopped, the sun began to climb over the horizon and, immediately, the air was loaded with fog as the heat from the red giant drew up the water soaking the ground.

These were not the best of conditions in which to ready the dwellings on Hightown for their rich occupants, rig the protective blowers, spray the area with strong fungicides, clear the landing field, sterilize the warehouses and do all the necessary things to make the station both attractive and safe.

"We'll have to get extra labor," he decided, "more men from Lowtown. We can issue them with the necessary clothing and they'll be glad to earn the money." He looked at the two men. "I don't suppose either of you would like to arrange it?"

"I'm busy," said Langel quickly, "too busy to go

into that stinking heap of filth."

"Sergi?"

"The same." The big engineer turned his head, concentrating on something to one side. "Trouble," he said. "I'll be seeing you, Factor."

Fuming, Meoud walked away, fighting his rage, and the mist, the mud, the very elements of Scar. The men hadn't really refused and, if they had, he lacked the power to make them venture into Lowtown in the spring. It was obvious that neither intended to leave the safety of the station area.

Ahead, hugging the edge of the landing field, he saw the outlines of a small portable church. Despite the streaming fog a line of men waited before the entrance. Cynically he watched them, knowing they queued less for spiritual balm than for the wafer of concentrates given as the bread of forgiveness after they had done subjective penance beneath the benediction light.

"You need help, brother?"

Meoud turned and stared at a figure in a rough, homespun robe. The cowl was rimmed with beads of water, the bare feet in their sandals coated with grime, but there was nothing pitiful about the figure. Brother Glee, while not a big man in the physical sense, was spiritually a giant. He stood, patiently waiting, the chipped bowl of crude plastic empty in his hand.

Meoud glanced at it. "No luck today, Brother?"

"None has as yet given charity," corrected the monk quietly. "Spring, on Scar, is a time of labor and, in such times, men tend to forget their less fortunate brethren."

"And at other times, too," said Meoud flatly. He raised his eye screen and squinted at the indistinct shape standing before him. "Why?" He said. "I've offered to let you eat at the canteen at my expense, and you could use one of the prefabricated huts as a church. Is it essential for you to live as animals in the mud?"

"Yes," said Brother Glee simply. "You are a kindly man, Factor Meoud, but in many ways you lack understanding. How could we dare preach to the unfortunate if we did not share their misery? How could they trust us, believe in the message we carry?"

"All men are brothers," said Meoud. "I don't wish to mock you, Brother, but there are many who would not agree with your teaching."

"That is not our teaching," said the monk patiently. "It is 'Do unto others as you would have them do unto you': the golden rule and the logical one of any thinking, feeling man. Look at them," he said, turning to gesture to the patiently waiting line. "Think of one thing, Factor Meoud. *There, but for the grace of God, go I!* Remember that and all else will fall into place."

He did not gesture with his bowl. The factor was primed and in a condition to give, but to force him to donate would be the result of pride, pride in the successful arrangement of an emotionally-loaded argument. There was another reason; Brother Glee was too good a psychologist to press his advantage. A donation now could have a later backlash. No man likes to think that he has been used or maneuvered.

"I need men," said Meoud suddenly, "strong men who are willing to work under orders. They will receive full rations for each day they work."

"And pay?"

"Equal to double rations," said Meoud. It was no time to haggle. "Treble rations for each man for eight days." He looked at the eyes shadowed by the cowl. "It is enough?"

"Would you work for such a sum after being starved all winter?"

"Yes," said Meoud firmly, and believed it. "If I were starving I would work for food alone."

"So you say, brother; but have you ever starved?"

"No," admitted the factor. "Food while they work and pay enough to buy food for three days more each day they work. I can do no more, Brother; you must believe that."

"I believe it," said the monk. "And, brother, we thank you."

The man was small and round, with a sweating face and an anxious expression. He wore a pointed cap and his wrists and ankles showed ruffs of yellow. His pants and blouse were of cerise striped with emerald, "Sir!" he called. "A moment, sir! Your attention, if you please."

Dumarest paused, casually interested. Farther down the line, a man lowered his hand, his face bleak as he turned to his wares.

"You are a man of discernment," babbled the vendor. "I could spot that in a moment, the way you entered, the way you walk. You are no stranger to this world, sir."

His voice was shrill with a peculiar penetrating quality which demanded attention. He stood before his wares, which were spread on one of the display stands in the station building. Both bar and canteen were fully operational now and the tables and chairs were fully occupied. Spring was leading to summer and a feverish excitement tinged the air.

Dumarest straightened and caught sight of Ewan busy with his shells. Men freshly awakened from deep sleep clustered around him and the air was full of the low buzz of conversation.

"Sir!" The vendor plucked at his arm. "Your attention for but a moment." His other hand picked up a shimmering heap of plastic. "Look at this suit, sir. Have you ever seen anything as light? Completely acid-proof, and that is only the start. Acid, fire, rot, spore, mold and fungus: nothing can penetrate this special material. Feel it, sir, handle it. I would appreciate your opinion."

Thoughtfully Dumarest examined the suit. It was light and flexible, a shimmering glory in his hands. Ignoring the actual material, he tested the seals and looked at the compact mechanism between the shoulders.

"The seals are guaranteed to withstand fifty atmospheres of pressure either way and yet can be opened with a touch. The filters are of triple construction and set in three distinct places. The absorption material can contain sixty times its own weight of perspiration. Dressed in one of these suits, sir, you could penetrate deep into the most parasitical growth of fungi on the planet."

"Have you tried it?" asked Dumarest.

The vendor frowned. "How do you mean, sir?"

"Have you tested it personally?"

The man smiled. "But, naturally, sir. How else could I offer it for sale with a genuine assurance that it will do everything I claim? I have worn it for five days under facsimile conditions and—"

"But not on Scar," interrupted Dumarest. "You haven't actually used it on a field expedition?"

"On this world, sir, no," admitted the vendor. "But the suit is fully guaranteed. You have absolutely nothing to fear."

"I see," said Dumarest. He frowned at the mechanism riding between the shoulders. "What would happen if I fell and buried my shoulders deep in mud?"

"The air-cell would continue to work under all conditions, sir."

"And suppose, at the same time, a fungi exploded and coated me with dangerous spores?"

"The filters would take care of that. Spores down to microscopic dimensions would be caught in one or the other of the treble filters. I am perfectly willing to demonstrate the suit under any conditions you may select, sir."

"Do that," suggested Dumarest. "Wear one and follow an expedition; test it as they order. If you remain alive and well you may possibly sell them—next year."

The vendor gave a pained smile. "Surely you jest, sir?"

"No," said Dumarest flatly. "I am perfectly serious. It is you who must be joking to ask men to buy your suits and risk their lives on your unsupported word. These men," he gestured to the other sellers of suits, "live here; they know the conditions. They know they will have to answer for every malfunction of any suit they sell, to the buyer or to his friends. Before you can hope to compete with them, you must equal their reputation."

Dropping the suit, he moved to where the man

who had lifted his hand waited. "Hello, Zegun, you looked worried. Has he been stealing your business?"

"Not yet, Earl, but when you showed interest I was anxious." Zegun picked up one of his suits. "He's a smart talker with a flashy line of goods. Cheap too. I can't begin to get near him."

"You don't have to," said Dumarest. "Not until he changes his design. With the filters where he has them and the air cell way back on the shoulders, it's impossible for one man alone to change either the filters or the battery. If the cell does keep working no matter what that isn't important, but who wants to risk his life on a thing like that?"

"No one," said Zegun emphatically. "I'll pass the word. You ready to be suited up now?"

"Later," said Dumarest. "Keep me one by."

He walked on, moving through the crowd, catching the vibrant air of expectancy which pervaded the place. It was always like this just before summer; men would boast a little, make plans, find partners and try to learn from those who had been there before.

A buyer stood on a low platform calling for those willing to sign up with his organization. He offered the basic cost plus a percentage of what was gained but neglected to stress that the basic cost had first to be met before profits could be earned. If a man worked hard and long, he could just make enough to last until the next season.

Another offered a guaranteed sum against a deposited investment.

A third knew exactly where to find a clump of golden spore.

Deafened by the drone of voices, Dumarest

passed through the vestibule and out into the fog. It was thinning now, the ruby-tinted mist dissolving beneath the growing heat of the swollen sun. It hung just over the horizon, a monstrous expanse of writhing flame and dull coruscations spotted with black penumbra. It was dying as Scar was dying, as the universe was dying. But Scar and its sun would be among the first to go.

He turned and walked to where the screaming whine of blowers tore the mist to shreds. A cleared space opened before him beyond the fans and the neat paths and colored domes of Hightown, each dome interconnected so that it was possible to stay completely undercover. Men wearing heavy clothing walked the paths with their sprays.

Suddenly restless, he turned to the landing field. Already the ships were arriving loaded with stores, supplies, exotic foods and manufactured goods. There were people too: the hard-eyed buyers, entrepreneurs, entertainers, vendors of a dozen kinds, young hopefuls intent on making a quick fortune and old prospectors unable to stay away.

There were travelers also, those who were willing to ride on a low passage doped, frozen and ninety percent dead, risking the fifteen percent death rate for the sake of cheap travel. A few would be lucky; many would not live through the summer; most would end in Lowtown, human debris at the end of the line.

"The fools!" said a voice behind him. "The stupid, ignorant fools! Why do they do it?"

"For adventure," said Dumarest. "Because they need to know what lies beyond; because it's a way of life." He turned. "Your way of life, Clemdish. How else did you come to Scar?"

Clemdish was a small wiry man, barely coming up to Dumarest's shoulder, with angry deep-set eyes and a flattened nose. He scowled at the ship and the handful of travelers coming from it.

"I was cheated," he said. "The handler lied; he told me the ship was bound for Wain." His scowl deepened. "Some people have a peculiar sense of humor."

"You were lucky," said Dumarest. "He could have cut the dope and let you wake screaming." He stared at the advancing group. The chance of seeing someone he knew was astronomically small, but they were his kind, restless, eager to keep traveling, always on the move.

"Fools," said Clemdish again. "Walking into a setup like this. How the hell do they expect to get a stake? They're stranded and don't yet know it." He rubbed at his nose. "But they'll find out," he promised. "Crazy fools."

"Shut up," said Dumarest.

"You feel sorry for them?" Clemdish shrugged. "Then go ahead and hold their hands, wipe their noses, give them the big hello."

"You talk too much," said Dumarest, "and mostly about the wrong things. Have you anything fixed for the summer?"

"Why? Are you offering me a job?"

"I could be. Interested?"

"If you're thinking of prospecting, then I'm interested," said Clemdish. "On a share basis only. If you're thinking of taking wages, then I don't know. Something else may come up, and it's certain that you'll never get rich working for someone else." He tilted his head as something cracked the sky. "What the hell—"

A ship dropped down from space, held by the magic of its Erhaft drive, aimed arrowlike at the field below. Clemdish whistled.

"Look at that, Earl! A private if ever I saw one! How much money do you need before you can own your own ship?"

"A lot," said Dumarest.

"Then you're looking at real money." Clemdish narrowed his eyes. "What's that blazoned on the hull? Some crazy pattern, but I can't quite make it out. It's familiar though; I've seen it before."

"In a deck of cards," said Dumarest wonderingly. "I've seen it too; it's a joker."

Together they watched the ship as it came to rest.

Chapter Three

Jellag Haig rested cautiously on the edge of his chair and looked thoughtfully at his goblet of wine. It was a deep blue, sparkling as it swirled in its crystal container, reflecting the light in sapphire glitters.

"Our own vintage," said Jocelyn, "from mutated berries grown under rigid control. I would appreciate your opinion."

The trader settled a little deeper into his chair. He was expected to flatter, of course. It was not every day that he was the guest of royalty, but he was experienced enough to know that a wise man never criticized his superiors, certainly not when they had invited him into their vessel, not when there seemed to be a strong possibility of doing business.

Carefully he waved the goblet beneath his nostrils, exaggerating the gesture a little but not enough to make it an obvious farce. The wine had a sharp, clean scent, reminiscent of ice and snow and a polar wind, with an undercurrent of something else which eluded him. He tasted it, holding the tart astringency against his tongue before allowing it to trickle gently down his throat.

It was unnecessary to flatter.

"My father worked for ten years to perfect the formula," said Jocelyn as he poured the trader more wine. "He based it on an old recipe he found in an ancient book and I think he made something in the region of a thousand experiments before he was satisfied. We call it Temporal Fire."

Jellag raised his eyebrows. "For what reason, my lord?"

"You will find out," promised Jocelyn. He smiled at the trader's startled expression. "You see? The full effects are not immediately apparent. Young lovers find the vintage particularly suited to their needs. Would you care for more?"

Jellag firmly set down his goblet. "I crave your indulgence, my lord, and your understanding. At my age such wine is to be avoided."

"Then try this," Jocelyn put aside the bottle and lifted the decanter filled with a warm redness. "You will find this acceptable, trader. That I promise."

Jellag sipped at the wine, wishing the he were elsewhere. *These high-born families and their inbreeding!* But they had power, power aside from the money power he himself possessed. He blinked. The wine was the local product colored into visual strangeness. He sipped again and wondered what else had been added aside from the dye. There was nothing that he could determine, but that meant little. He relaxed as his host drank, refilled his goblet and drank again.

"You prefer this vintage, trader?"

"It is more familiar, my lord." Jellag gulped the wine, a little ashamed of his suspicions and eager to show he had no mistrust. "But the other is amusing; it would make an ideal jest."

Jocelyn smiled. "You appreciate a jest?"

"I have a sense of humor, my lord." Jellag felt it safe to claim that. He drank a little more, conscious of a faint carelessness, a disturbing lightheadedness. Had something been added to the wine, some subtle drug to which his host had the antidote? He watched as ruby liquid ran from the decanter into his goblet. "With respect, my lord, may I ask what brings you to Scar?"

"Destiny."

Jellag blinked. "My lord?"

"The workings of fate." Jocelyn leaned forward in his chair, his eyes hard as they searched the trader's face. "Do you believe in destiny? Do you believe that, at times, some force of which we are not wholly aware directs our actions, or, rather, presents us with a choice of action? At such times what do you do?" He did not wait for an answer. "You guess," he said, "or you ponder the improbables and do what you think best. The wise man spins a coin." He lifted the decanter. "More wine?"

Jellag sucked in his cheeks. Had he been invited aboard simply to act as drinking companion to a madman? *No,* he thought, *not mad. Odd, perhaps, strange even, but not mad.* The rich were never that.

"I spoke with the factor," said Jocelyn smoothly. "I wanted the advice of a man who knew his business. He told me that you were such a one. How long have you been coming to Scar?"

"Many years, my lord."

"And you make a profit?"

Jellag nodded.

"How?"

Jellag sighed. "I buy and I sell, my lord," he said patiently, "rare spores if they are available, useful ones if they are not. Scar is a world ripe with fungoid growth," he explained. "Each season there are mutations and crossbreedings without number. Many of the products of such random blending are unique. There is a sewage farm on Inlan which is now a rich source of food and valuable soil. Spores from Scar were adapted to that environment, fungoids feeding on the organic matter and turning waste into rich loam. On Aye other spores are cultivated to produce a hampering growth on voracious insect life." Jellag spread his hands. "I could quote endless examples."

"I am sure you could." Jocelyn frowned thoughtfully. "I owe you an apology," he said. "I thought you were an ordinary trader, but clearly I was wrong. You are an expert in a specialized field, a mycologist. I take it that you have to grow and check, breed and test the various spores you obtain?"

Jellag was reluctant to be honest. "Not exactly, my lord. The season on Scar is too short for me to test in depth; I rely on my laboratory to do that. But when I arrive, I have a shrewd idea of what to look for: spores which will develop growths of minute size so as to penetrate invisible cracks in stone, to grow there, to expand, to crush the rock into powder; others to rear as high as a tree to provide shade for tender crops; still more to adjust a planet's ecology; edible fungi of a hundred different varieties; parasitical growths with caps containing unusual drugs or stems from which products can be made; molds which act as living laboratories; slimes which can be grown to need. The economy of a world could be based on the intelligent use of fungi." Jellag blinked, wondering at his feeling of pride. *And yet, why should I not be proud? A specialist! A builder of worlds!*

Jocelyn leaned forward and poured his guest more wine. "You are a clever man, my friend. You would be most welcome on Jest."

"Thank you, my lord."

"Most welcome," repeated Jocelyn meaningfully. "I am a believer in destiny. It seems as if fate itself directed me to this world." He sipped his wine, eyes enigmatic as he stared over the rim of his goblet. "You have a family?"

"A wife and two daughters, my lord. The eldest girl is married, with children of her own."

"You are fortunate to have grandchildren. They, too, are fortunate to have so skillful a grandfather, a man who could do much for his house." He lifted his goblet. "I drink to your family."

They'll never believe it, thought Jellag. *The ruler of a world drinking to their health!* His hand shook a little as he followed Jocelyn's example; courtesy dictated that he empty the goblet. Politeness ensured that, in turn, he found the boldness to return the toast.

"Now, my friend," said Jocelyn lifting the decanter. "Tell me more about your fascinating profession."

Adrienne stormed into her cabin, her nostrils white with anger and her eyes glinting in the hard pallor of her face. "The fool!" she said. "The stupid, besotted fool!"

"My lady?" Her maid, a slender, dark-haired girl cowered as she approached. She had unpleasant memories of earlier days when her mistress had vented her rage in personal violence.

"Get out!" Adrienne hardly looked at the girl. "Wait! Tell cyber I wish to see him. Immediately!"

She was brushing her hair when Yeon entered the cabin. He stood watching her, his hands as usual hidden within the sleeves of his robe and his cowl thrown back from his shaven skull. The brush made a soft rasping sound as it pulled through her hair; it was almost the sound of an animal breathing, a reflection of her inner self. Abruptly, she threw aside the brush and turned, facing the silent figure in scarlet.

"You were advisor to my father," she said. "Is it you I have to thank for being married to a fool?"

"My lady?"

"He's down there now in the lower cabin drinking with a common trader; he's praising him, toasting his family, promising him ridiculous things. My husband!" She rose, tall, hard and arrogant. "Has he no dignity, no pride? Does he regard the rule of a world so lightly?"

Detached in his appraisal, Yeon made no comment, watching her as she paced the floor. No one could have called her beautiful and spoken with truth. Her face was too thin, her eyes set too close, her jaw too prominent. Her figure was angular, though clearly feminine, as if she deliberately cultivated a masculine stance. The long strands of her hair hung about her shoulders, loose now, but normally dragged back and caught at the base of her skull. Her mouth alone was out of place; the lower lip was full, betraying her sensuousness.

"Why?" she demanded. "Why, of all men, did my father have to pick him?"

Yeon moved a little. "Your genetic strains are highly compatible, my lady. Both your husband

and your father were most insistent on this point; both agreed that, above all, the union should be fertile.''

"A brood mare to a fool, is that all I am?" Rage drove her across the floor and back again, the metal heels of her shoes tearing at the fine weave of the carpet, her hair swirling to glint ashen in the light. Abruptly she halted, glaring at the cyber. ''Well?''

"You wish me to answer, my lady?"

"Would I have asked if I did not?"

"No, my lady." Yeon paused and then, in the same even monotone said, "You are the wife of the ruler of a world, a queen. Many would envy you your position."

"Are you now saying that I should be grateful?" For a moment it seemed as if she would strike the enigmatic figure in scarlet, and then, as if coming to her senses, she shuddered and lowered her up-raised arm. "I am distraught," she said unevenly, "unaware of what I was doing. I apologize for any offensive behavior."

Yeon bowed. "No apology is necessary, my lady. No offense was taken." He watched as she returned to the seat before the mirror. "You disturb yourself needlessly. Against the major pattern, the trifles of which you complain are meaningless. I would advise you to ignore such petty irritations."

Her eyes stared into the mirror and found his reflection there.

"Before agreeing to the marriage contract," the cyber continued, "your father asked me to predict the logical outcome of the proposed union. I must admit that my answer was hampered by lack of knowledge of Jest. A true prediction can only be based on assured fact."

She turned, her face tilted up at his shaven skull. "Continue," she ordered, remembering veiled hints Elgone had dropped and which she had been too busy or too annoyed to understand. "What was your prediction?"

"You will have a child, a son. Failing other offspring of your family—and the genetic forecast promises none—that child will inherit the rule not only of Jest but also of Eldfane."

She frowned. The family was inbred, she knew; but she did not think it that infertile.

"It is a matter of the direct line," said Yeon, guessing her thoughts. "Those of a station suitable for union with either of your two brothers are incompatible. The laws of Eldfane do not recognize the issue of unregistered unions, and your father will never consent to accept a commoner as the legal wife of either of his sons. Therefore, your child must be the logical heir of both worlds."

Sharp white teeth bit thoughtfully at the fullness of her lower lip. The future prospects of her unborn son were bright, but what about herself? Yeon remained enigmatic.

"Once the child is safely conceived, my lady, many things can happen. I hesitate to do other than touch on possibilities."

"Jocelyn could die," she said harshly. "One way or another, he could be disposed of. I would still remain Queen of Jest."

"Perhaps, my lady."

"There is doubt?"

"There is always doubt. New laws could be passed to take care of that eventuality, perhaps old ones already exist. I have still to assimilate much data appertaining to the world. It would be wise to move with caution."

"To wait, you mean, to act the dutiful wife, and, while waiting, to be the laughing stock of all who see the conduct of my husband. Destiny," she snapped. "How can a grown man be such a fool? How can he hope to retain the rule of his world? Has he no nobles weary of his antics?" Rage lifted her once more from the chair and sent her striding the floor. "Did you hear him when he decided to head for Scar, his talk of omens and signs sent by fate? Can such a man be allowed to rule?"

"Do not underestimate him, my lady. Many men wear a mask to hide their thoughts."

"Not my dear husband, cyber," she said bitterly. "I know more than you. He is what he appears to be." She frowned, her anger dissipating as she considered her future. Yeon was right, it would be ill-advised to act prematurely. First she would have to make friends, gain sympathizers and, above all, ensure the conception of her child.

That, at least, should not be difficult.

Dumarest paused and looked up at the low range of peaked hills, their sides scored and gullied, masses of exposed stone looking like teeth in a rotting mouth.

"There's nothing up there," said Clemdish. He eased back the wide-brimmed hat he wore and mopped at his streaming face. Overhead, the monstrous disk of the sun glowed with furnace heat. Even though it was barely summer the temperature was soaring, a grim promise of what was to come. "I tried it once," he continued, "the first season I was here and damn near killed myself climbing to the top. It was a waste of time. There's nothing beyond; just the reverse slope running down to the sea."

"I'd like to see it," said Dumarest.

Clemdish shrugged. "Who's stopping you?" The small man looked around, found a rock and sat down. "I've gone far enough. It's a waste of effort, Earl. The wind is from the sea all the time, and any spores will be blown back inland. We'd do better scouting farther back this side of the range."

Dumarest ignored him, concentrating on the hills. If he were to take the gully up to where it joined a mesh of shallow ruts, swing left to hit that crevasse, ease himself along until he reached a jutting mass of stone and then edge right again, he shouldn't have much difficulty in making his way to the top.

He turned at the sound of a soft thud. Clemdish had slipped off his pack and was rummaging through its interior. He looked up defiantly.

"I'm hungry," he said. "I figure on taking time out to rest and eat. You going to join me?"

Dumarest shook his head. "I'm going to take a look at what's beyond those hills. You wait here and guard the packs." He undid the straps of his own and dropped it beside the one Clemdish had thrown down. "Go easy on the water; It's a long way back to the station."

"Too damn long," grumbled the small man. "Coming this far out was a crazy thing to do. It's bad enough now, what's it going to be like later?" He scowled after Dumarest as he moved away.

"Hey, don't forget your markers."

Dumarest smiled. "I thought you said it was a waste of time?"

"I still think so," said Clemdish stubbornly. "But take them just the same." He threw a couple of thin rods at Dumarest. "Sling them over your back, and Earl."

"What now?"

"Be careful."

"What else?"

"I mean it," insisted Clemdish. "You're a big man, heavy. I don't want to bust a gut carrying you down. Remember that."

The first part of the climb wasn't very difficult. Dumarest followed his memorized route and paused as he reached the mass of stone to catch his breath. The temptation to strip was strong, but he resisted it. The sun was too big, too loaded with harmful radiation. Invisible infrared light could burn a man before he knew it, and there was always the chance of a random spore. Clothing might not keep them out, but it forced the body to perspire and so would wash them from the flesh.

He edged right, cautiously testing each foothold before applying his full weight, gripping firmly with both hands as he moved along. The sun-baked surface was treacherous, the soil beneath weakened by the winter rains and ready to crumble at any misdirected impact. Higher it wasn't so bad, for masses of stone, leached from the dirt, formed a secure matrix; he covered the remainder of the journey at fairly high speed.

Resting on the summit of a peak, he looked around.

The view was superb.

Looking back the way he had come he could see the scarred plain rolling towards the horizon, the rough ground interspersed with patches of smoothness where the trapped ooze of winter had firmed during the spring. They looked darker, richer than the rest, and countless buds of wakening growth dotted them like a scatter of snow. Other growths, less advanced, showed wherever bare dirt faced the sky. In the shadow of rock, molds and slimes stretched as spores multiplied and grew in the mounting heat.

Small in the distance, Clemdish sat with his back against a rock, his legs sprawled before him and the packs resting to one side beneath the protection of one arm. Dumarest shaded his eyes with the edge of his hand. Farther back, almost invisible against the faint haze still rising from the ground, the tiny, antlike figures of scouting men could be seen as they swung in a circle around the station. The landing field itself was below the horizon, since Scar was a dense but small planet.

Dumarest turned and felt the soft touch of a breeze against his perspiring face. From where he stood the ground fell sharply away in an almost sheer drop before it eased into a gullied slope running down to the sea.

There was no sand and no shore as such. The winter rains which had lashed the high ground for aeons was gradually washing the soil and rock into the sea. A sullen red beneath the sun, its surface was broken only by the occasional ripple of aquatic life, calm in the knowledge that, given time, it would spread over the planet in unquestioned domination of the entire world.

Dumarest moved and a rock, loosened by his

foot, fell tumbling, bouncing high as it hit stone
and rolling until it dropped over the edge of the
cliff and fell into the sea. Ripples spread, shimmering in shades of crimson and scarlet, dull maroon
and glowing ruby, the colors fading and blending
as the disturbance spread, the tiny waves dying at
last.

He turned, looking back to where Clemdish sat
sprawled in sleep, and then looked back at the sea.
With one slip he could easily follow the rock. A fall
could break his leg or send him tumbling from the
cliff.

Carefully, he lowered himself down to where a
boulder thrust from the dirt, a temporary resting
place. Budding growths thrust smooth protrusions
to either side, and Dumarest smiled at the evidence
of his suspicions. The wind was from the sea, but
released spores had been driven back against the
side of the hill rather than carried over the summit.
Better still, if the wind was steady the spores would
be driven back to their original sites. The chance of
scattering with the resultant crossbreeding would
be diminished. Logically here, if anywhere on Scar,
the fungi would breed true.

Dirt showered from beneath a foot as he moved
and he froze, feeling sweat running down his face,
fingers like claws as he gouged at the soil. More
dirt shifted; a small rock fell. There was a sudden
yielding of hardened surface, a miniature
avalanche, gathered momentum as it slid towards
the cliff.

Dumarest rolled, his muscles exploding into a
fury of action as he released his grip and threw
himself sideways to where a rock thrust from the
slope. He hit it, felt it shift beneath his weight and

threw himself still farther, rolling as the stone joined the showering detritus. He choked on the rising dust, rolled again and spread arms and legs wide in an effort to gain traction. Desperately he snatched the knife from his boot and drove the blade to the hilt in the ground. It held, and he clung to it, trying to ease the strain on the blade, rasping his booted feet as he fought to find purchase.

Beneath him the sea boiled with the shower of falling stones and dirt.

The knife held. His boots found something on which to press. The fingers of his free hand dug and found comforting solidity. The dust dissipated and, after a long moment, he lifted his head and looked around.

He hung on the edge of a sheer drop, his feet inches from where moist soil showed the meshed tendrils of subterranean growth. To one side showed more wet earth, graying as it dried beneath the wind and sun. Above lay apparent firmness.

He eased towards it, moving an inch at a time, pressing his body hard against the dirt so as to diminish the strain. His boots stabbed at the mesh of tendrils, held, and allowed his free hand to find a fresh purchase. He crawled spiderlike up the slope to comparative safety. Finally, knife in hand, he reached the secure refuge of a shallow depression in a circling cup of embedded stone.

His face down, he fought to control the quivering of his muscles, the reaction from sudden and unexpected exertion. Slowly the roar of pulsing blood faded in his ears and the rasp of his breathing eased, as did the pounding of his heart. He rolled and looked at the knife in his hand, then thrust it at his boot. He missed and tried again, this

time stooping to make sure the blade was in its
sheath.

He stiffened as he saw the cluster of hemispheres
at his side.

They were two inches across, marbled with a peculiar pattern of red and black stippled with yellow. He had seen that pattern before. Every man at
the station had seen it, but it was essential to be
sure.

Dumarest took a small folder from his pocket. It
was filled with colored depictions of various types
of fungi both in their early stages of growth and at
maturity. He riffled the pages and found what he
wanted. Holding the page beside the hemispheres
at his side he checked each of fifteen confirming
details.

Slowly he put the book away.

It was the dream of every prospector on Scar. It
was the jackpot, the big find, the one thing which
could make them what they wanted to be. There
were the rare and fabulously valuable motes which
could live within the human metabolism, acting as
a symbiote and giving longevity, heightened aware-
ness, enhanced sensory appreciation and increased
endurance.

There was golden spore all around him, in a
place which he had almost died to find.

Clemdish lifted his head his eyes widening as he
looked at Dumarest. "Earl, what the hell happened
to you?"

He rose as Dumarest slumped to the ground. His
gray tunic, pants and boots were scarred; blood

oozed from beneath his fingernails; his face was haggard with fatigue.

"I told you not to go," said Clemdish. "I warned you it was a waste of time. What the hell happened? Did you fall?"

Dumarest nodded.

"You need food," said the little man, "water, something to give you a lift." He produced a canteen; from a phial he shook a couple of tablets and passed them to Dumarest. "Swallow these; get them down." He watched as Dumarest obeyed. "I was getting ready to come after you. Man, you look a wreck!"

"I feel one." Dumarest drew a deep breath, filling his lungs and expelling the vitiated air. The drugs he had swallowed were beginning to work; already he felt less fatigued. "I fell," he said. "I went down too far and couldn't get back. The surface was like jelly. It refused to support my weight."

"It wouldn't." Clemdish dug again into his pack and produced a slab of concentrates. "Chew on this." He watched as Dumarest ate. "I tried to tell you," he reminded. "I told you climbing those hills was a waste of time. You could have got yourself killed, and for what?"

Dumarest said nothing.

"You've lost your markers too," pointed out the little man. "Not that it matters. We've got plenty more, too damn many." He scowled up at the sun. "A waste of time," he muttered. "Too much time."

"All right," said Dumarest. "You've told me. Now forget it."

"We can't," said Clemdish. "We daren't. We've

got to get back before it gets too hot."

He rose from where he sat and kicked at a clump
of mottled fungi. Already the growths were much
larger than they had been when Dumarest began
his climb. The entire land surface of the planet was
literally bursting with life as the growing heat of
the sun triggered the dormant spores into development. The pace would increase even more as the
summer progressed, the fungi swelling visibly in
the compressed and exaggerated life cycle of the
planet.

To the visiting tourists it made a unique spectacle. To the prospectors and those depending on the
harvest for their living it meant a dangerous and
nerve-racking race against time.

Dumarest ate the last of the concentrate, washing it down with a drink of tepid water. He lay
back, his face shadowed against the sun, feeling the
twitch and tension of overstrained muscles. The
journey from the place where he had found the
golden spore had been a nightmare. The ground
had yielded too easily and he'd been forced to
make a wide detour, fighting for every inch of upward progress. By the time he had reached safety,
he had been practically exhausted.

Then had come the downward journey, easier
but still not without risk. Fatigue had made him
clumsy, and twice he had taken nasty falls. But
now he was safe, able to rest, to relax and feel the
ground firm and stable beneath his back.

"Earl!"

Dumarest jerked, suddenly conscious that he
had drifted into sleep.

"Earl!" It was Clemdish. "Earl! Come and look
at this!"

He was standing well over to one side, a mass of
fungi reaching halfway to his knee; those were
twisted, tormented growths, striped with puce and
emerald. He called again as Dumarest climbed to
his feet.

"What is it?"

"Something good, I think. Come and check it
out, will you?" Clemdish waited until Dumarest
had joined him and then pointed. "That's a
basidiomycete if ever I saw one. Worth collecting,
too. Agreed?"

Dumarest dropped to his knees and examined
what Clemdish had found. Ringed by the puce and
emerald growths was a group of spiraloids of
cream dotted with flecks of brown and topaz, the
whole cluster seeming to be the towers of some
fairyland castle. He reached into his pocket and
withdrew the folder. It was already open to show
the pictures of golden spore. He flipped the pages
until he found the information he wanted.

"You're right," he told the little man. "This one
is worth money. We'd better mark it and clear the
area."

He swept his boot across the surrounding
growths as Clemdish returned to the packs for one
of the thin rods. He thrust it close beside the cluster
of spirals. Around the rod was wrapped a ten-foot
length of thread and the top was split so as to hold
a card marked with their names. All the ground
within the compass of the thread was theirs to
harvest.

Clemdish joined Dumarest in clearing away the
unwanted fungi to give the selected growth more
room to develop.

"That should do it," he said. "Our first claim.

Unless someone steals our marker," he added, "or switches cards, or gets here before we do."

"You're a pessimist," said Dumarest.

"It's been known," insisted Clemdish. "You should know that. Some of the boys last season swore that someone had shifted their markers. If they find him, he'll never do it again." He looked at the sun and ran his tongue over his lips. "Let's get moving," he suggested. "You all right now, Earl?"

"I can manage."

"We'll head directly back," said Clemdish. "Cut a straight line from here to the station. If we see anything good we'll mark it, but we won't stray from the route. We can come out later," he added, "when you've had a chance to get some rest. Run a circle close to the station and check out a couple of spots I know. You agree, Earl?"

Dumarest nodded.

"Then let's go. I'll take the lead."

"Just a minute," said Dumarest. "There's something you should know." He looked at the other man. "We've found the jackpot," he said quietly. "There's a clump of golden spore on the other side of the hills."

Clemdish sat down, his legs suddenly weak.

Chapter Four

Heldar felt the gnawing pain in his chest, the scratching irritation and the liquid demanding release. He coughed; the initial expelling of air triggered a bout of hacking which left him weak. Grimly, he looked at the red flecks staining his hand.

The small, round vendor with the ruff of yellow at wrists and ankles looked at him with sympathy. "You need help," he said. "Why don't you see a physician?"

Heldar grunted. The station had no resident medical technician, only a snap-freeze cabinet where the severely injured could be held in stasis and the deep-sleep facilities, which could be adapted to promote healing. All else had to wait until a traveling physician arrived to ply his trade. Such doctors had a strict order of priority: money came first. Heldar had to raise a loan.

Craden shook his head when Heldar mentioned it. He was new to Scar, but was far from inexperienced. Casually he inspected one of the yellow ruffs circling his wrist, "You work for the company, don't you? Wouldn't they make you an advance?"

"Zopolis wouldn't lend his own mother the price of a meal," said Heldar viciously. He had already tried and been refused. The pain in his chest mounted and he coughed again. When he recovered he looked frightened. "It's killing me," he gasped. "What the hell can I do?"

The vendor inspected his other ruff. "Beg," he suggested. "What else?"

Heldar left the room and stood blinking in the glare of the sun. It seemed to cover most of the sky with the glowing fury of its disk, but that was an optical illusion. It was big, but not that big. If it had been Scar would long ago have shattered into a ring of debris.

He coughed again. The chest pain was getting worse as it grew hotter and there was still more heat to come. Heldar reached back to where his hat hung from his neck on a thong and drew it over his eyes. Beg, Craden had advised. But from whom? The monks had nothing but the barest essentials. The factor couldn't give what he didn't have, and neither he or anyone else would make what would have to be an outright gift of money.

He stared over the field, seeing the ships waiting to carry their passengers home and others discharging people in order to get away. They were commercial, and, if they carried a physician at all, he would be exactly the same as the one in Hightown. There was only one chance, the small, private vessel with the peculiar insignia. It carried royalty and would be certain to have a physician. *Maybe, if I'm humble and pile it on?* He coughed again and spat a mouthful of blood; there would be no need for pretense.

*   *   *

"Sit down," said the doctor. "Relax. Throw your head back until it touches the rest. Farther. That's right. Now just relax."

Gratefully Heldar did as ordered. He felt euphoric, still unable to believe his luck. *Coincidence,* he told himself. *I just managed to see the right man at the right time, the boss man himself. I hit the right button and he did the rest.*

He heard metallic tinklings behind him and resisted the desire to turn. The doctor's voice was flat and indifferent.

"Do you wish to stay, my lord?"

"Will you be long?"

"For the examination? No, my lord."

"Then I will stay," said Jocelyn. He looked down at the patient's face. "You have nothing to worry about," he soothed. "Just do as Erlan tells you to do."

Erlan, thought Heldar, *the physician. And the one who just spoke is the boss man, the ruler of Jest. But where were the courtiers? The guards?* He felt the desire to cough; then something entered his mouth and sent a spray down his throat, killing the desire. He tensed.

"Relax," said the doctor sharply. "Constriction of the muscles does not ease my task."

Something followed what had contained the spray. Seemingly huge, it slid down his throat, probing past the windpipe. There was a soft hissing, and abruptly he lost the sense of feeling from his mouth to his lungs. Wider tubes followed; he could tell by the mechanical dilation of his mouth.

"I have expanded the path to the lungs, my lord," said Erlan, as if commenting to a colleague. "Now we pass down the light, so, and swivel, so."

He drew in his breath. "A classic case," he murmured. "Extreme erosion of the junction together with scarification of the trachea and widespread seepage." His voice faded as he manipulated more instruments. Metal scraped on crystal. Heldar felt something tickle deep in his chest, then the tube was withdrawn from his throat and another spray returned feeling to the numb areas.

Automatically, he coughed.

"Some wine?" Jocelyn extended a glass filled with amber glintings. "Sip," he advised, "your throat is probably a little tender."

"Thank you, my lord." Heldar sat upright and turned his head. Erlan sat at a microscope studying a slide. As he watched he changed it for another and increased the magnification.

"Well?" said Jocelyn.

"There is no doubt, my lord." Erlan straightened from his instrument and casually threw both slides into an incinerator. A flash of blue flame converted them both to ash. "The man is suffering from a fungous infection, obviously parasitic and of some duration. It could have been caused by a single spore which has increased by geometrical progression. Both lungs are affected, the left almost hopelessly so, and the inevitable result, unless there is surgery, is death."

Heldar gulped his wine, oblivious of the sting to his throat.

Jocelyn was gentle. "Therapy?"

"The infection is aerobic. It would be possible to seal and collapse one lung and coat the area infected of the other with inhibiting compounds. The capability of respiration would be greatly reduced; the patient would have to rest with the minimum of effort for at least a year."

"The alternative?"

"Complete transplants, my lord, either from an organ bank or from new organs grown from the patient's cells. The former would be quicker, the latter more to be preferred, but in both cases a major operation coupled with extensive therapy is unavoidable."

"But he would live?"

Erlan sounded a little impatient, "Certainly, my lord, the operation would be a matter of routine."

"Thank you," said Jocelyn. "You may leave us." He turned and poured Heldar more wine. "You heard?"

"Yes, my lord."

"And understood?" Jocelyn was insistent. "I mean really understood?"

"Unless I receive an operation I shall inevitably die," said Heldar, and then added, "my lord."

Jocelyn sighed. "Exactly. I wanted to be sure you fully comprehended the situation. I can, of course, arrange for you to have the necessary treatment but there are conditions."

"Anything," blurted Heldar, "anything at all, my lord."

"You would come with me to Jest under restrictive indenture?"

Heldar nodded. What had he to lose? "When?" he asked. "The treatment, my lord, when would it be given?"

"That," said Jocelyn softly, "depends entirely on yourself; not as to when, of course, but whether or not it will be given at all." He reached behind him to where the wine stood on a table. A coin rested beside the bottle. He picked it up and tossed it to Heldar. "Look at it," he invited. "It will decide your fate."

"My lord?"

"On one side you will see the head of a man. I have scratched a line across his cheek, a scar. The other side bears the arms of Jest. Spin the coin. Should it fall with that side uppermost you will receive your needed treatment, but if the other side should be uppermost, the scar, then you belong to this world and I will not help you."

Heldar looked at the coin, then raised his eyes. "My life to depend on the spin of a coin? My lord, surely you jest?"

"No," said Jocelyn, "I do not jest." His voice hardened. "Spin!"

The coin rose, glinting, a blur as it climbed to hesitate and fall ringing to the deck. Jocelyn glanced at it, his face expressionless. Unbidden, Heldar rose, crossed to where it lay and looked down at the shining disk. He felt the sudden constriction of his stomach.

"Luck is against you," said Jocelyn quietly. "It seems that you are fated to die."

The interior of the shed was cool with a brisk crispness which stung like a shower of ice, refreshing as it hurt, waking senses dulled with seemingly endless heat. Kel Zopolis paused, enjoying the coolness, and then, remembering the cost, walked quickly down the shed.

"Wandara!"

"Here, Boss." The overseer came from behind a machine, wiping his hands on a scrap of waste, his white teeth flashing against the ebon of his skin. "The cooling plant is switched off," he said before the agent could raise the matter. "I was just testing the machines to make sure they'll work when we want them."

"And?"

"Fully operational," said the overseer, "hoppers, slicers, balers, everything." He walked beside Zopolis down the length of the shed and opened a door, waiting for the agent to pass through before following him and closing the panel.

Beyond lay a second shed filled with equipment. A line of rafts, each with a thousand cubic feet of loading capacity, rested against one wall. Suits, boots, masks and sprays hung neatly on hooks. A heap of wide-bladed machetes rested on a bench beside a grinding wheel. They were thirty inches from pommel to point, the blades slightly curved and four inches across at the widest part. Zopolis lifted one and swung it, enjoying the heft and balance of the well-designed tool.

Wandara spoke as he tested the edge.

"I'm sharpening them up, Boss, giving them a real, fine edge. They'll cut through any fungus on the planet."

And more than a swollen stem, thought the agent, as he replaced the machete. He remembered a time two seasons back, or perhaps three, when two crews had fallen out, each accusing the other of cheating. Then the machetes had been used as swords. Even now he could remember the mess, the blood and the cries of the wounded.

"The rafts," he said. "I want them all ready to operate within five hours."

"They're ready now, Boss." Wandara sounded hurt. "You didn't think I'd play around with machetes if the rafts needed checking?"

"No," said Zopolis. *Pride,* he thought. *I've hurt his pride.* Aloud he said, "I'm sorry. It was foolish of me to ask."

The overseer grunted, mollified. "Starting to harvest, Boss?"

"Soon. I'm taking a survey to check the state of the crop. If it's ready we'll start right away. In any case, you can pass the word that we'll be needing men."

"Sure, Boss. The same terms?"

"Piecework, yes, but we've got to cut the price by five percent." Zopolis didn't look at the other man. "It isn't my doing," he said. "I'm just following orders. It's a reduction all along the line."

"The processing sheds too?"

"Yes, but we'll reserve those jobs for the weak and incapable." *The ones who've starved too much and too long,* he thought, *the ill, the chronically sick, the dying.* "I'll have a word with Brother Glee about that. He'll know who to pick." He glanced sharply at the overseer. "Something on your mind?"

"Heldar, Boss, I don't want him around."

"Why not? He's a regular."

"He's trouble. There's talk of someone moving claim markers and stealing original finds. I don't figure on letting him use our rafts and our time for his own business."

"He was on scout duty," mused Zopolis thoughtfully. "It would give him the opportunity. Do you think he's guilty?"

Wandara shrugged. "I don't know, Boss. He could be; he knows a lot about electronics and could rig up a detector. I just don't want him around."

"Ground him," decided the agent. "Put him to

work here in the sheds. Give him three days; and if he starts to loaf, get rid of him."

Leaving the overseer, he walked down the shed to where the door stood open. He opened it still more and stepped outside. The sun was nearing its zenith and the heat was stifling. The dull red light of the sun stained the ground, the buildings and the faces of those walking about the station, so that it seemed they all lived in a giant oven.

He caught a glimpse of motion and turned. A raft was rising from Hightown, anti-gravity plates robbing it of weight and the engine sending it silently through the air. Beneath a transparent canopy, a cluster of tourists sat in air-conditioned comfort. They were all looking downward at the weird forest of colorful growths spreading all around the station to the limits of visibility.

Zopolis sighed, envying them a little. They could sit and watch and wonder at the fantastic configurations of the exotic fungi, at their monstrous size, endless variety and incredible rate of growth. He had to test and judge and select the exact moment to commence the harvest. It it were too early, the crop would lack flavor, if too late, there would be no time to gather the quantity needed to make the operation a financial success. The fungi would reach maturity, produce spores, lose quality, and, worse, perhaps be contaminated by harmful elements.

Not for the first time he wished that he had taken up a different profession.

The entertainment had been discreetly advertised as a program of strange and unusual practices of a cultural nature collected on a score of primitive worlds. To Adrienne it was a monotonous collection of boring filth.

The whippings didn't disturb her and neither did the flayings, cuttings, scarification of tender organs and feats of drug-assisted endurance; Eldfane had hardened her to the spectacle of pain. On that rough world, punishment was public and, if any sightseers gained an erotic satisfaction from the spectacle it was an unintentional bonus. To her, pain was meant to hurt and nothing else. As for the rest, she grew impatient with the sighs and inhalations of the others crowded in the small auditorium. Surely there was nothing strange about sex.

Impatiently she turned, searching for her maid. The girl sat with her eyes enormous, her moist lips parted and her body twitching in time to the hiss and crack of the whip. Colors from the three-dimensional representation flowed over her flawless skin and touched her dark hair with shimmers of rainbow brilliance.

"Keelah!"

The girl blinked. "My lady?"

"Attend me!" Adrienne rose, careless of the comfort of those to either side and careless of those she thrust aside on her way to the exit. The anxious entrepreneur bowed as she approached.

"My lady, I trust the performance did not offend?"

"You did ill to invite me," she snapped. "The factor will hear of this, and," she added, "it would not be wise for you to visit either Jest or Eldfane. My father has a way of dealing with vermin of your kind."

"My lady?"

"Stripped," she said brutally, "castrated,

blinded and released in the streets as sport for the mobs."

Regally she swept through the corridors of Hightown. A scarlet shadow detached itself from a bench and fell into step at her side.

"Do you return to the ship, my lady?"

She did not look at the cyber. "You have some other suggestion?"

"A raft could be hired if you wish to see Scar. The growths at this time of the season are extremely interesting. The visual aspect, too, is most unusual."

With an effort she restrained her temper, remembering who the cyber was and what he represented. The Cyclan was quick to avenge any injury or slight done to its members.

"Thank you, Yeon, but no." Spitefully she added, "Have you any other suggestions?"

"There are always the information tapes on Jest, my lady."

Irritably she thinned her lips, half suspecting him of irony. Surely he must know that she was in no mood for education. A guard at the exit bowed as they approached, opened the first door and bowed again as they passed. There were two more doors and a second guard stood before the final barrier. As they passed into the open air a man flung himself at her feet.

"My lady! Of your charity, save a dying man!"

She stepped back, suddenly fearful. Assassins had been known to adopt strange disguises.

"Please, my lady!" Heldar raised distorted features to her. "A word with your husband on my behalf—a single word!" His voice rose as she stepped farther back. "At least let me spin again! It is my life, my lady, my life!"

"What is this?" Anger replaced her fear. Where were the guards, the retinue without which one of her station should never be without. "Who are you?"

Yeon stepped between the grovelling suppliant and the woman. "Attend your mistress," he said to the girl and then he said to Adrienne, "My lady, do not concern yourself; the man is distraught. With your permission, I will attend to the matter."

She nodded and swept towards the ship, fuming with rage. *I, the queen of a world, to be treated so! And still Jocelyn refuses to leave this backward place. Still he insists on playing his stupid games, making his stupid promises and talking all the time of destiny and fate.*

But there was one thing at least she could do.

"Quick-time?" Jocelyn rose from his chair as she burst into his cabin with her demand. "Are you so bored?"

"I am."

"But there is so much to see. You could visit Lowtown—Ilgash will accompany you—or inspect the village around the station. We could invite the factor and a few others to a meal, and surely Hightown has something to offer in the way of entertainment."

She was insistent. "I did not leave Eldfane to be stranded on this apology of a world. You seem able to amuse yourself, but I cannot. I see no pleasure in walking through slums, eating with commercially-minded fools or watching unsavory images. I refuse to suffer longer because of your whims."

"Suffer?" Jocelyn stepped close and looked into her eyes. "Are conditions so unbearable?" he asked softly. "I had the impression that we were on our honeymoon. There are many ways, in such circumstances, to alleviate the slow passage of time."

"Must you talk like a peasant!" Memory of the recent entertainment brought a red flush to her cheeks. "There will be time enough to conceive an heir after we land on Jest. Until then, I demand to be spared further humiliation. At least quick-time will shorten this interminable period of waiting. I shall, of course," she added, remembering the girl's nubile beauty, "expect Keelah to attend me."

Jocelyn frowned, understanding the innuendo, and his face grew hard. "I am sorry. It would not be convenient at this time to grant your request."

She looked at him, eyes wide with incredulous anger.

"You are my wife," he said. "As such, your place is by my side. Because things are a little tedious, do you imagine that you can escape them by running away? His voice was a hammer driving home the point it was essential to make. "Jest is not a soft world, Adrienne. There is much that will prove tedious and unpleasant but will have to be faced. I suggest that you begin to learn the basic elements of self-discipline."

He was being unfair and knew it. Eldfane, also, was not a soft world; but the aristocracy had cushioned themselves against its natural harshness by becoming encysted in ritual and formality. Now, as his wife, Adrienne expected to be the head of such a world within a world. It was best to disillusion her now.

Training helped her to contain her anger. "You are well named," she said coldly, "but I do not appreciate the jest. Neither, do I think, will my father."

He bridled at the threat. "You wish to break the

contract? Let me warn you that, if you do, you will not be welcome at your father's house. He has too many daughters still unwed. Why else do you think he was so eager to give me your hand?"

Immediately he repented of his cruelty. "Adrienne," he said, softly. "I did not marry you simply for your dowry, nor because we are genetically compatible and should have no trouble obtaining issue. I married you because—"

"You needed a wife to breed more fools," she interrupted savagely, "a woman to bring you goods and credit and the loan of trained and intelligent minds. Well, you have those things, but do not expect to gain more. And do not expect me to aid you with your insane projects. I do not relish being the butt of lesser folk. I, at least, have dignity."

"And can you live on that? Her rejection sharpened his rage. "You dislike slums, but are there no slums on Eldfane? You sneer at commercially-minded fools, but who else is to plot our prosperity? Unsavory images are only what you make of them and, in any case, who are you to either judge or condemn?" He fought his anger, drawing air deep into his lungs and wondering where his sense of the ridiculous had gone. Now, above all, he needed the soothing balm of humor. "Scar is a backward world," he said. "There is no industry here, no real population, certainly no ruling class. These people will mostly be gone at the end of summer and we shall, most probably, never see any of them again. So, my dear, why be concerned over your image?"

"Is pride a garment to be taken off and put

aside?" Her voice was thin and acid with dislike. "I gain no pleasure from this conversation. With your permission, my lord, I will retire."

He sighed as she swept from the room. *Women, who can gauge their emotions? Perhaps I've been wrong to deny her the use of quick-time. The hours drag and who knows what mischief a bored and idle woman might do? And yet she has to learn, accept the fact that life has to be lived, if nothing else.*

He sat down and picked up his book. He held it in one hand as he stared at the cover, but he did not see the stained and crumbling material beneath the plastic seal. He was thinking of other things. Jellag Haig for one. The trader was hovering on the brink of decision, a little more pressure and he would surely yield.

Thoughtfully, Jocelyn leaned back in his chair.

It would be best to make him a baron, he decided, to begin with, at least. Later, if he proved himself, he could be elevated to an earl or even a duke, but first he would be a baron.

Baron Jellag Haig of Jest.

It made a satisfying mouthful and would please his family. He would have an armorial crest together with a residence and an estate, a small residence and a big estate.

Land was cheap on Jest.

Chapter Five

Ewan sat at his table, deft hands busy as he manipulated his shells. The little ball bounded from one to the other, vanishing only to reappear and vanish again.

"A test of skill," he droned in his flat, emotionless voice. "Now you see it, now you don't. Pick the shell it is under and I will double your money. The more you put down the more you pick up. Why risk your neck when you can get rich the easy way? Hurry, hurry, hurry. Hit while the game is hot."

Like the room, he thought, *the station, the whole stinking planet.* Late summer on Scar was the anteroom of hell. He glanced around beneath hooded eyes, his hand moving mechanically and his voice droning its attention getting chant. No one took any notice; business was bad.

Business had been bad all through the season. There had been the usual flurry at the end of spring when those in deep sleep had awakened eager for a little excitement, but lack of a reliable protector had made him cautious. He'd been forced to play carefully, letting too many win too often, hoping to recoup later in the season.

Later could be too late. Those who had been lucky would be in a hurry to leave the planet, and those that hadn't would be conserving their money in order to pay for deep sleep or, if they lacked enough for that, hugging every coin to see them through to the next summer. A few would be desperate enough to take a risk, but they would have little to lose.

"Hurry, hurry, hurry," he droned. "Pick the shell with the ball and double your money. Step up and match the quickness of your eye against the swiftness of my hand." He scowled at the continuing lack of attention.

"You're getting good," said Dumarest. He walked from behind the gambler and sat down facing him. "Real good. You could almost pass for an honest man."

"I am an honest man," said Ewan. "I am exactly what I appear to be." He looked up, studying the other man. "You've been out a long time, Earl. Find anything good?"

Dumarest shrugged. "The usual. A few clumps which might pay enough to keep us going."

"You and Clemdish?"

"That's right."

Ewan nodded and then abruptly pushed away his shells. "I saw you when you came in," he said. "The pair of you. You both looked all in, but Clemdish was up and about some time ago. My guess is that you carried him, did all the work."

"You guess wrong," said Dumarest. "I'm not that stupid. If I take a partner, he does his full share." He changed the subject. "How's business?"

"Not so good." Ewan pursed his lips and leaned back in his chair. "I've had to work under a handicap. No protection," he explained. "And money seems to be tighter than ever. Have you heard the gossip?"

"About the ship with the joker?" Dumarest nodded. "I heard."

"A weird character," summed up the gambler. "But he isn't the only one." He leaned forward, lowering his voice. "Listen, if you've found anything really good, be careful; I mean extra careful. There's something odd going on, too many men hanging about for no obvious reason. I've seen it happen before. A lot of good men seemed to vanish about that time."

"Jumpers?"

"I don't know. But when a man comes back from harvesting what he's found, he's liable to be tired and a little careless. If someone was waiting for him, he wouldn't stand much of a chance."

"That's obvious," said Dumarest.

"Sure, it is, but if I can think of it, then so can others." Ewan reached out and touched his shells, moving them casually with the tips of his fingers. "There's a few of them in here right now."

Dumarest didn't move. "Where?"

"Over at the bar, the group in the far corner. And there's something else: I overheard someone talking about a ring." The shells made a little sliding sound as Ewan moved them from side to side. "A ring like the one you're wearing."

Dumarest frowned. "I don't get it. Why should they be interested in my ring?"

"I didn't say they were," corrected the gambler. "But there's one sure way to find out."

"Sometimes," said Dumarest, "you make pretty good sense."

He rose, smiling as if at a joke, and casually turned. Three men stood engaged in conversation, one of them looking in his direction. The man was a stranger. He crossed to where Zegun stood before his wares, and managed to catch a glimpse of the other two. Both were unfamiliar. None of the three bore any resemblance to the cat-man or his companion. They could have been entrepreneurs, minor traders, or belated prospectors, but Ewan knew his people.

"Hello, Earl." The vendor smiled his pleasure. "Glad to see you back. I was beginning to wonder if you'd had an accident. You were both out a long time."

"We took a good look around," said Dumarest. "One thing I'll say for Clemdish, he certainly knows how to live off the land. He even found some drinkable water."

"I know," said Zegun. "He's got a nose for it. He told me that you'd covered quite an area."

"Told you?"

"When he ordered your supplies," explained the vendor. "a few hours ago."

Dumarest kept his voice casual. "Maybe I'd better check his list."

"You're the boss." Zegun found a slip of paper. "Here it is; suits, spare filters, power cells, a couple of machetes, tent, collection sacks and storage containers, the usual equipment, rope too." Zegun looked curious. "I wondered about that. What the hell do you need rope for, Earl?"

Dumarest was bland. "We're going fishing," he said, "from a raft."

Zegun laughed. "Now I know you're joking. Every raft on the planet is booked solid. Even the tourist transport's locked up tight." He scowled, suddenly annoyed. "Something should be done about those fat slobs taking a man's living. They get a yen to go hunting, buy a suit and hire a guide and hope to find something to help pay expenses. But they've got to do it the easy way, they've got to ride."

"Why not?" said Dumarest. "Wouldn't you?"

"Sure," admitted Zegun. "But that doesn't make it right."

Clemdish looked down at his hands. "I'm sorry, Earl. I was only trying to help."

"By tipping our hand?" Dumarest walked three paces to the end of the cubicle, turned and walked back again. He halted, staring down at the man sitting on the edge of the bed. "Rope," he said. "Any idiot would guess from that that we'd found something in the hills. Why didn't you leave it to me to order the equipment?"

Clemdish met his eyes. "What difference would it have made? We still need rope."

"Maybe," said Dumarest. "I'm not so sure."

"Earl?"

"The golden spore is in a place almost impossible to reach. We've got to find it, harvest it and bring it back. The chances are that we won't even be able to get near it unless we've got a raft. Even if we do manage to collect it, our troubles won't be over."

"Jumpers?" Clemdish frowned. "We can take care of those."

"There's another way," said Dumarest, "a better way, perhaps. We sell the location to one of the traders, Zopolis, even. He has the men and equipment to handle it. While he's doing that, we can take care of our other finds."

"No!" Clemdish was emphatic.

Dumarest sighed. "Be reasonable. What's the good of money to a dead man?"

"We won't be dead," said Clemdish. He rose, trembling. "No," he said again. "I mean it, Earl. I'm your partner, and I've a right to my say. That golden spore is ours!"

Dumarest remained silent.

"We can't afford to deal with a trader," said Clemdish earnestly. "You know what will happen. He'll work on a contingent basis. Even if he believes you and makes a deal, it will be all his way. First he'll charge for the cost of harvesting, then he'll want his cut and more. If we get a fifth of its value we'll be lucky. That's a tenth each, Earl."

"I could make a better deal than that," said Dumarest.

"I doubt it. The traders have formed themselves into a combine so you have to play the game their way. But even if you did up the percentage, that's all it would ever be—a part when you could have the whole. Why should we give money away?"

Dumarest stared at his partner. "We won't be giving money away," he reminded. "We'll be collecting some trouble-free cash."

"The cost of a few high passages," said Clemdish bitterly. "And, when that's gone, what then? No, Earl. This is my chance to get rich, and I'm not letting any fat slob of a trader cash in on it. We'll get the stuff if I have to crawl naked down the side of a mountain."

He was shouting, the metal walls vibrating to his vehemence, his face ugly with passion.

"Calm down," said Dumarest.

"That golden spore is mine!" shouted Clemdish. "Half of it anyway. We're partners, and don't you forget it!"

"I'm not forgetting it," snapped Dumarest. "Now calm down. You want everone to know our business?"

"I—" Clemdish gulped, suddenly aware of his stupidity. "I'm sorry, Earl. It's just that I can't let that spore go. It's the chance of a lifetime, and I've got to take it."

"All right," said Dumarest.

"It's the thing I've dreamed about," said Clemdish, "the one real chance to make a break."

Dumarest nodded, suddenly feeling the constriction of the walls, the cramped confines of the little room. A bed, a locker and tier of drawers both fitted with thumbprint locks, a metered entertainment screen and a single chair were the entire furnishings of the cubicle. To Clemdish it was luxury. How could he be blamed for wanting to break free?

"Get some sleep," said Dumarest quietly. "Soak up as much water as you can; eat some decent food, and keep quiet," he added. "What's done is done, but there's no sense in making things worse."

He left before Clemdish could answer, striding from the little room, down the echoing passage and out into the open air. The sun hit like the blast of a furnace and he blinked, pulling the wide brim of his hat low over his eyes. Dust swirled from beneath his boots as he walked from the dormitory. To one side, on the edge of the landing field, someone had erected a wide awning. Shouts rose from a group of men as they watched two others wrestle.

They were crewmen from the waiting space ships, mostly, finding relaxation in primitive sport.

Wandara grinned with a brilliant flash of teeth as Dumarest approached the processing sheds. "Hello there, Earl, you come looking for work?"

Dumarest shook his head.

"That's a real pity. You'd make a good boss for one of the rafts, or would you like to go scouting? Top rates, and I won't bear down if you take time out to do some personal harvesting." The overseer winked. "Just as long as you remember old friends."

Dumarest smiled. "No thanks. I've got too much to do to work for basics. Ready for harvest yet?"

"Almost." Wandara turned to where a mass of fungi lay on a wide bench. Picking up a machete he hacked off a mass of liver-colored sponginess. "Brown glory," he said. "Tell me what you think."

Dumarest bit into the mass and chewed the succulent pulp. "Too early," he said. "The flavor still has to develop."

The overseer nodded. "Now this."

It was a mass of convoluted velvet spotted with blue and cerise. The texture was that of soft cake, the taste of a mixture of tart and sugar.

"About right," said Dumarest. He looked past the overseer to where the main processing shed stood closed. "Got all your staff yet?"

"We don't start them until we need them," said Wandara. "You know that. But Brother Glee is passing the word." He turned back to his bench, his machete glittering in the sun as he chopped the collected fungi to pieces for examination.

This batch was for testing and disposal. The rest

would be for slicing and dehydrating by a quick-freeze process which kept the flavor intact. It would be packed for the markets of a hundred worlds. Gourmets light years apart would relish the soups and ragouts made from the fungi harvested on Scar.

Dumarest turned away and headed for the awning. A man called as he approached.

"Try this delicious confection, sir, spun sugar touched with the juice of rare fruits!"

Another said, "See the mating dance of the Adrimish. Feel the sting of their whips, the touch of their nails: full sensory recording."

A stooped crone was next. "Cold drinks, my lord, iced to tantalize and tease the tongue."

The small-time entrepreneurs of Scar were taking full advantage of the boredom attending late summer. A man sidled close and spoke in a whisper.

"A half share in a clump of golden spore, yours for the cost of a high passage."

From one side a man droned as he stooped over a crystal ball filled with minute and swarming life.

"See the epic struggle of the sharmen as they battle with alien spores. Watch as they turn into mobile balls of destructive vegetation. The next show about to commence. Two places yet to be filled."

A woman laughed as she danced to the dull thudding of a drum, coins scattering around her naked feet.

A roar lifted from the center of the crowd. A man rose, stripped to the waist, struggling against the hands which gripped hip and shoulder. He spun, twice, then was dashed to the ground.

"Brother!"

Dumarest turned to face the monk, looked at the lined face beneath the shielding cowl. "Brother Glee, How can I help you?"

"Not I, brother, but one who claims to be a friend of yours, a woman of Lowtown. She has a scarred cheek and neck."

"Selene?" Dumarest frowned. "She sold me food and shelter."

"Even so, brother. She asked for you."

"Why? Is something wrong?"

The monk nodded. "Of your charity, brother, will you come?"

She looked very small huddled on her bed of rags. The scar was hidden and, with her cropped hair, she seemed more like an adventurous boy than a mature woman who had seen too much of the hard side of life. Then she turned and Dumarest could see the rags and blood and the damage done to the side of her head.

"Earl?"

"Here." He found her hand and gripped it. "What happened?"

"Earl." Her fingers tightened. "I'm frightened, Earl. It's so dark, and it shouldn't be dark, not in summer, not like this."

Dumarest raised his head and looked at the monk standing on the other side of the bed. Brother Glee spoke before his junior could answer Dumarest's unspoken question.

"We were selecting those for work in the sheds of agent Zopolis. "Men and women in the greatest need. Selene was one. We entered and found her lying in a pool of blood; she had been struck down."

"Why?"

"I do not know, brother," said the monk quietly. "But it was rumored that she had money hidden away."

Dumarest turned, looking at the interior of the hut. The corner which had held his bed was a jumbled mess. The chests had been wrenched open; scraps of fabric littered the floor. Even the plastic fragments lining the sagging roof had been torn down. Someone had searched the place with a furious desperation.

"Earl." Her voice was a fading whisper. "It's so dark, Earl, so dark!"

"The blow crushed the side of her head," said the junior monk quietly. "She is paralyzed down one side and totally blind. I have managed to staunch the bleeding, but there is extensive damage to the brain." He paused and then added, "There are other minor injuries: bruises and lacerations together with burns."

"Torture?"

The monk inclined his head. "It would appear so; she was gagged when we found her."

Dumarest leaned closer to the woman on the bed. "Selene," he said urgently. "Who did it? Tell me who did it."

Her fingers closed even tighter on his. "Earl," she breathed, "You came, I needed you and you came."

"Who did it?"

"A man," she said. "He wanted money."

"Which man? Did you know him? Tell me his name."

"Name?" She moved a little. "Hurt," she said, whimpering. "He hurt me."

"The damage to her brain has obviously impaired her memory," said the junior monk softly. "It could be that she is unable to tell you more."

"She must." Anger made Dumarest curt. "A woman," he said, "harmless, trying to make a living the best way she could—and some money-hungry swine comes to her home and does this to her." He stooped even lower over the bed, his lips almost touching her ear. "Selene!" he said sharply. "Listen to me."

"Earl?"

"You must tell me who the man was. Who did this to you?"

She moved a little as if trying to escape from something unpleasant.

"Tell me," he insisted.

"Rings," she said abruptly. "Rings!" Then, with a fading softness, she continued, "Earl, don't leave me. Earl . . . don't leave me."

He felt the fingers locked on his own suddenly relax, watched as the cropped head turned, falling on the crude pillow, hiding the scar for the last time.

Dumarest rose, stepping back as the monk gently closed her dead eyes and turning to face the silent figure of Brother Glee.

"You came here looking for her," he said. "Did you see anyone leave as you approached? Someone who stood close to the hut, perhaps, or who may have passed you on the path."

Beneath the shadow of the cowl the eyes of the monk were steady on his own. "What do you intend, brother?"

"I am going to find the man responsible for this," said Dumarest tightly. "He will not do it again."

"Murder, brother?"

"Justice, monk, the only kind of justice there is on this planet. Or do you wish to see the man who did this escape?"

Brother Glee shook his head. Dumarest was right. There was no law on Scar, no police or other authority which had any interest in what had happened. But, if he should prove too hasty, what then?

"There was a man," said the monk softly. He would suffer penance for this later; it was not his place to speak when his superior remained silent. But he was young and not yet divorced from anger. "A contract man; Heldar."

"Heldar," said Dumarest slowly. He had heard the gossip. "He was close?"

"He passed us on the path."

"Alone" said Brother Glee quickly. The damage was now done; all he could do was to minimize the probable consequences. "And there is no proof. We saw nothing to connect him with the crime."

"Have no fear, Brother," said Dumarest curtly. "I shall not harm an innocent man."

The crowds had thickened at the fair when Dumarest returned. A girl caught his arm; her face was dotted with luminous points and her hair a frizzled mass of silver and gold.

"Hello, handsome," she cooed. "Why look so grim?"

He shook free his arm and pressed deeper into the crowd, his eyes searching.

Another girl, a blonde with tattooed lips, pressed her lush body against his chest. "How about me giving you something nice, good looking?" Her smile was inviting. "Nice clean sheets, full stimulating apparatus and something to get you into the mood. Satifaction guaranteed, or a full refund." She tilted her head to where a space ship, blazoned with phallic symbols, stood close by. "Yes?"

"No."

"Impotent?" she snapped, then lost her sneer as she saw his face.

He ignored her, pressing through the crowd and using the advantage of his height. A man like Heldar, frightened perhaps, would find comfort in a crowd; he would not like to be alone until his nerves had settled. Yet he wasn't at the fair. *The station, perhaps?*

Dumarest strode through the dormitories, not finding the man he sought. He could be lurking somewhere in Lowtown, though it was doubtful, or the sheds, perhaps.

Wandara shook his head. "No, Earl, I can't say that I've seen him. Is it important?"

"Yes," said Dumarest. "Do you mind if I have a look round?"

"Sure," said the overseer, "help yourself."

The interior of the shed was silent, shadowed with equipment. Dumarest walked slowly down the center, his eyes probing to either side. Heldar could have entered by the door to the rear of where

Wandara had been working. He heard a soft rustle, the sound of movement.

"Heldar?"

It came again. It was the sound of fabric sliding against metal, as if a man were squeezing himself between the end of a raft and the wall of the shed.

"Come out," said Dumarest. "If I have to come after you, you'll regret it."

"What you want?" Heldar blinked as he came from between two rafts. "I was catching a nap; you woke me up. What's all this about?"

"Come outside," said Dumarest. "I've got something to tell you." Casually he led the way to where Wandara stood at his bench. The overseer looked up and laid down his machete.

"Find him?"

"I'm here." Heldar stepped into the sunlight. "I still want to know what all this is about."

"A woman was murdered down in Lowtown," said Dumarest curtly. "I think you did it."

"You're crazy!"

"You were seen!"

"That's a lie!" Heldar looked at Wandara. "I've been here for the past five hours, asleep in the shed. How the hell could I have murdered anyone?"

"Just a minute," said the overseer. He looked at Dumarest. "So a woman's been murdered," he said. "So what business is it of yours?"

"She was a friend of mine."

"That's different," said Wandara. "You're lying." he said to Heldar. "This shed was locked tight until three hours ago."

"So I misjudged the time," said Heldar. "But why blame me if a woman got herself killed? I had nothing to do with it."

"The woman was hit over the head," said Dumarest. "She bled quite a lot. You've got some of it on your boots."

Heldar looked down, then up, his eyes frightened. "I didn't do it."

"There's an easy way to find out," said Dumarest gently. "The witness could be wrong. All you have to do is to go to the church and get under the benediction light." he explained. "The monks are good at finding out the truth."

It was by hypnosis, naturally, with the swirling mass of kaleidoscopic colors from the benediction light a perfect tool for the purpose. If Heldar was innocent there was no reason why he should refuse.

"All right," he said. "I'll do it."

He walked past Dumarest towards the landing field, where the portable church was almost lost among the milling crowd. He reached the bench, the spot where the overseer had laid down his machete. As he passed he picked it up and, spinning in a blur of motion, swung it at Dumarest.

Automatic reflex saved him. He ducked and felt the blade slice off the crown of his hat. He jumped back as Heldar advanced and felt the point rasp across his chest, laying open the plastic and baring the protective mesh beneath. Then Wandara moved in, trapping Heldar's arm and twisting it until he dropped the blade.

"Hell," he said, "If you want to fight, do it properly."

It was an excuse for a spectacle. Dumarest felt the sun on his bare head as men rushed to make a circle, the avid faces of women appearing at their sides, the dust slowly settling as volunteers attended to the formalities.

"You'll have to strip, Earl!" His ebon face gleaming with sweat, Wandara looked to where Heldar was baring his chest. "He's good," he warned. "I've seen him fight before. Watch out for an upward slash on a backhand delivery; he twists the blade at the last moment."

"I'll watch out for it," said Dumarest.

"He's got a trick of dropping and slashing at the ankles, too." Wandara took the proffered tunic and threw it over his arm. "Do you really think he killed that woman?"

"Why else did he attack me?"

"I heard about it," said Wandara. "The poor bitch! Don't let him get away with it, Earl." He handed over a machete. "I'll have to take your knife."

Dumarest nodded, handed over the weapon and stepped forward, swinging the machete to get the feel of it. It was too long and clumsy for comfort. At the far side of the ring Heldar was accompanied by the men Dumarest had seen at the bar. They took his tunic and slapped him on the back.

"All right," said Wandara. His voice rose above the babble and brought silence. "This is between these two; anyone interfering can have his chance later." He looked from one side of the ring to the other. "It's all yours. What are you waiting for?"

He ducked away as they advanced, the scuff of their boots loud in the silence.

It was a silence Dumarest had heard before; the bated breath of watchers hungry for the sight of blood and pain, eager to taste the vicarious thrill of hacking a man to death. It hung over the crowd like a miasma, merging with the brooding heat of the sun, adding to the mounting tension so that men clenched their hands until the nails dug into their palms and women chewed orgiastically at their lower lips.

"Earl," said Heldar as he approached. "There's no need for this. What the hell can you gain by killing me?"

Dumarest advanced, poised on the balls of his feet, the machete gripped so as to reflect the sun from the polished blade.

"I've got nothing to lose; I'm dying anyway," whispered Heldar. "Maybe you'll do me a favor by making it quick."

His arm sagged a little, the gleaming blade lowering its point to the dirt, almost as if the weight was too great for his hand. It flashed with reflected sunlight, flashed again and then seemed to disappear.

Dumarest sprang to one side and felt the wind of the blow against his upper left arm. Immediately he slashed, a blow level with the ground at waist height, drawing back the blade in a slice.

He felt the shock and jar of a parrying blade, the rasp of steel racing towards his hand and swung his own blade in a swinging counter-parry. Heldar grinned as he forced continuance of the motion, throwing Dumarest's machete to one side and opening his defense. Sunlight sparkled in rainbow shimmers as his blade hissed through the air, cutting through the spot where Dumarest had stood, snarling at the lack of impact.

Again he rushed to the attack, and again Dumarest saved himself by a quick retreat. Heldar was good, fast and clever with the blade, moving with the unthinking speed of automatic reflex, using the sun itself to disguise the movements of his machete as he caught and lost the blinding reflection. Steel rasped, scraped with a nerve-grating sound and hummed with diminishing vibrations. Dumarest felt something touch his upper arm. He spun, stroked with the blade and saw a gush of red appear at Heldar's side.

The man turned, ran to the far side of the circle and turned with his free hand dabbing at the wound. He advanced again and, as he came within range, threw a handful of blood at Dumarest's eyes. At the same moment he dropped and brought the machete around in a whining blur at his ankles.

Dumarest sprang to one side and upwards, The blade passed beneath his feet. Before Heldar could recover, he swept down with his blade. There was a sound as of an ax hitting wood. From the assembled crowd came the hissing intake of breath.

"He's done it!" Wandara yelled as he jumped into the circle. "Cut his head damn near right off! Dumarest wins!"

Dumarest thrust his machete into the ground and stooped over the dead body. From a pocket he took a scrap of rag. Opening it, he stared at five rings, each with a red stone.

"Is that what he killed her for?" Wandara shook his head. "For a handful of lousy rings?"

Dumarest said bleakly, "No, for his life."

He walked to where Brother Glee stood at the edge of the crowd. "Here," he said, and gave him the rings. "Take them, for charity."

Chapter Six

Jocelyn lifted his glass. He said, "A toast, to all who love justice!"

Dumarest touched his lips to the blue wine. Across the table Del Meoud suddenly spluttered, dabbing hastily at his beard. Dumarest caught Adrienne's look of displeasure and her husband's wry grimace. Jellag Haig laughed with amused condescension.

"The factor finds such a toast hard to swallow," he said. "There is little justice on Scar."

"And less mercy!" The factor was sharp. "And who makes it so? There are traders who care nothing how they make their profit, nor how men are turned into beasts in the scrabble for wealth."

Jocelyn waited as a servant refilled the glasses. "You are too hard on Baron Haig," he said quietly. "Is a man to blame for the system? If he is wise, he uses it. If he is foolish, he allows it to use him." He looked at Dumarest. "You fought well," he said. "Would I be wrong if I said that you are no stranger to the arena?"

"I have fought before," said Dumarest.

"Often?" Adrienne leaned forward across the

table; her eyes were bright with anticipation. "Tell us about it."

"I fight only when necessary, my lady, when there is food to be earned, my life to protect or a friend to avenge. There is no pleasure in blood for those who fight."

She frowned, disappointed. On Eldfane man fought as a profession, and most of them seemed to enjoy the activity and the rewards. She said so. Dumarest met her eyes.

"You are speaking of entertainment, my lady. Some men may enjoy killing and may even wish to die, but I am not one of them. A fight, to me, is something to be ended quickly. You cannot afford to play with a man who seeks your life."

"But Heldar—"

"Was a fool," he said brusquely. "He depended on tricks to win. When a trick fails there is no defense. He should have relied on skill and speed."

"As you did. You were fast," she admitted. "We could see it all on the scanners. But if you find no pleasure in battle, why seek it? What was Heldar to you?"

"He killed for money; but, with respect, my lady, he was not wholly to blame."

She looked at him, waiting.

"He was dying," explained Dumarest. "He knew it. A dying man has nothing to lose. Had he not lost the spin of a coin he would be alive, the woman would be alive and we should not be sitting here drinking to a thing called justice."

"You do not like the word?"

"My lady, I do not. I would prefer to drink to a thing called mercy."

He had gone too far. He could tell it from the

tension which had closed around the table, the way Haig refused to meet his eyes, the way the factor fumbled at his beard. A guest should never insult his host. The more so when that host is the ruler of a world. But they were not on Jest. They were sitting in Jocelyn's ship on a free planet and Dumarest had too recent memories; a cropped head turning to hide a scar, staring eyes which could not see, the pressure of a hand, a man made desperate because of a ruler's whim.

There had been blood on the dust and a body lying sprawled in the sun.

Meoud coughed and glanced at his timepiece. "My lord, I crave your indulgence and permission to depart; there are matters to which I should attend without delay."

"You may leave," said Jocelyn. "You also, Baron. We shall talk again later."

"My lord." Jellag Haig rose. "My lady." He bowed to them both. "My thanks for a wonderful meal." He bowed again and followed the factor from the cabin. The sound of their footsteps died as the door closed behind them.

"Wine," ordered Jocelyn. The gush of liquid from the bottle sounded unnaturally loud. He waited until all three glasses had been refilled, then picked up his own. He said, "A toast, to justice!"

Dumarest set down his empty glass.

"Tell me about yourself," said Jocelyn abruptly. "The factor tells me that you search for a dream, a legendary planet. Is that true?"

"Earth is no legend, my lord. I was born there, I know."

Adrienne frowned. "But in that case, surely you would know where it is. Could you not find it by merely retracing your journey?"

"No, my lady. I left when I was very young," he explained. "Ten years of age. I stowed away on a ship. The captain was kinder than I deserved; he should have evicted me but he was old and had no son. Instead, he kept me with him. From then on, it was a matter of traveling from world to world."

"Always deeper into the heart of the galaxy," mused Jocelyn, "where the worlds are close and journeys short. Until perhaps, you probed into the far side from the center." He nodded. "I can appreciate the problem. Can you, my dear?"

Adrienne sipped her wine, her eyes on Dumarest as she tasted the blue stimulant. He was tall and hard with a face of planes and hollows, a firm mouth and strong jaw. His was the face of a man who had learned to live without the protection of house or guild, a man who had learned to rely on none but himself.

She looked at her husband. He was not as tall, not as broad; he had russet hair, a sensitive face, delicate hands and an old-young look around the eyes. But he too, she realized with sudden insight, had learned to rely on none but himself. But, where Dumarest had an impassive strength, Jocelyn used the mask of ironic humor.

"Adrienne?"

She started, aware that Jocelyn waited for an answer. "I can appreciate many things," she said ambiguously. "But does not each man have his own problem?"

"Philosophy?" Jocelyn looked at his wife with wondering eyes. "You betray hidden depths, my dear."

"Only to those with the wit to plumb them, my lord." The wine, she realized, was affecting her senses. The recent fight too had stimulated her, so that she was uneasily conscious of the proximity of men. Firmly she set down her glass. "Shall we move into the lounge, my husband? The remains of a meal is not the most attractive of sights."

Yeon rose as they entered the lounge, a flash of scarlet against the lined walls and worn furnishings. He looked at Dumarest as if sensing his dislike, then looked at Jocelyn. "Do you wish me to depart, my lord?"

"Stay," said Jocelyn carelessly. "You may be able to help us with a problem."

The cyber bowed and resumed his chair. A viewer stood on a small table before him, a rack of tapes to one side. While the others had eaten, he had studied. Food, to Yeon, was a matter of fuel for his body. He could neither taste nor enjoy the varied flavors savored by normal men.

"You spoke of a problem, my lord?"

"A matter of extrapolation," said Jocelyn. He smiled as Adrienne passed a tray loaded with delicacies. Deliberately, he chose and ate a compote of crushed nuts blended with wild honey. "How long would it take a man to visit each world?"

"Each habitable world, my lord?"

"Yes."

"It would depend on the route," said Yeon carefully. "If the journey was that of a spiral starting from the outer edge of the galaxy and winding in towards the center it would take many lifetimes. If the journey was done in reverse it would take almost as long, but not exactly because of the galactic drift which could be turned to some slight advantage. It—"

"Would take longer than a man has reason to think he will live," interrupted Jocelyn. He helped himself to another sweetmeat. "That does not aid us, cyber. If you were to seek a planet, the coordinates of which you neither knew nor could discover, how would you go about it?"

"I would accumulate all available information and from that extrapolate a probable locality." The cyber maintained his even modulation despite the apparent pointlessness of the question. "The mathematics of random selection could, perhaps, be used to advantage; but I must inform you, my lord, the problem verges on the paradoxical. To find a place the location of which is unknown is surely an impossibility."

"Improbability," corrected Jocelyn. "In this universe nothing is impossible."

"As you say, my lord." Yeon looked sharply at Dumarest. "May I ask if the problem has some personal significance?"

"Yes," said Jocelyn. "Earl," he looked at his guest. "I may call you that? Thank you. Earl is looking for his home world, a planet called Earth. Of your skill and knowledge, cyber, can you aid us in the matter?"

"The name means nothing to me, my lord. Would there be a description?"

Dumarest said, "A scarred place, a large, single moon in the sky. The terrain is torn as if by ancient wars. Life is scarce, but still ships call and leave again. They serve those who reside deep in caverns.

The sun is yellow. In winter there is cold and snow."

Yeon shook his head. "It means nothing."

Adrienne carried the tray to Dumarest and offered it for his selection. "Try one of the fruits," she suggested, "The texture is of meat laced with wine, blue wine. I think you will appreciate the combination."

"Thank you, my lady." His insult, apparently, had been wholly forgiven, but still he did not completely relax. There were undercurrents of which he was uneasily aware. But the sweets seemed harmless enough. He chose and ate. As she had promised, the combination was pleasing.

"Take another," she urged. "Several. I weary of acting the servant." Putting down the tray she sat down, her long legs somehow ungraceful, her hair an ashen cascade. "Tell me," she demanded. "What do you think of our vessel?"

Dumarest leaned back, glad of the opportunity to be openly curious. To one side, Jocelyn and the cyber conversed in low tones. Beyond them, lining the walls, ancient books rested in sealed frames. The carpet and chairs were old and the small tables scattered about bore an elaborate inlay which could only have been done by hand.

He looked up at the ceiling. It was vaulted and groined in an archaic style which belonged more to an edifice of stone than to a vessel designed to traverse space. It was a clue which had eluded him and made everything fall into place.

"Well?" Adrienne was watching him with her bright eyes, her cheeks flushed a little as if from inner excitement.

"It is strange, my lady," said Dumarest slowly. "I have never seen such decoration before in a space ship. It is as if someone had recreated the interior of a study belonging, perhaps, to some old stronghold."

"A museum," she said, suddenly bitter. "A collection of worthless rubbish."

"Far from worthless, my lady," corrected Dumarest. "There are those who would pay highly for such items."

"Lovers of the past," she said. "But what is the use of that? The past is dead, only the future remains of importance."

My future, she thought. *With my son heir to both worlds, myself as his regent. Jocelyn's. Or was that so essential?*

She looked at Dumarest, conscious of his strength and determination. He had courage, and that was a quality admired on Eldfane. Her father would have lifted him high—or broken him on the wheel for having dared to say what he had. Jocelyn? Only he knew what thoughts coiled in his brain. Did he consider it a jest? Would his peculiarities descend to his child?

Dumarest met her eyes. "The future, my lady, is the result of the past. As the child is the fruit of the father, so today is the child of yesterday. Actions done today have their effect tomorrow. That is why there are many who respect what has gone before."

"Pour me wine," she demanded. Had he been able to read her thoughts? "The green wine, not the blue. Join me if you will."

He leaned across the small table and lifted the decanter. Red fire shone from his ring as he passed her a glass. "That ring," she said abruptly. "A gift?"

Dumarest nodded.

"From someone special? A woman?"

He looked down at it, rubbing his thumb over the stone. "Yes, my lady," he said quietly, "from someone very special."

A mane of lustrous red hair, eyes like sparkling emeralds, skin as soft and white as translucent snow.
Kalin!

"Rings?" Jocelyn turned from the cyber. "Is there a mystery about them? The man you killed, Heldar, and rings also. Where did he get them?"

"From the woman he killed, my lord." Dumarest was curt.

"And she?"

Dumarest shook his head. "I do not know. Gifts, perhaps; who can tell?"

"They had red stones," said Jocelyn thoughtfully. "I saw them after you had given them to the monk. Is there something special about such rings? If so, then be wary, my friend." He rose from where he sat. "You are excused, cyber. Adrienne, I think it time you retired."

Dumarest rose together with the scarlet figure.

"Not you, Earl," said Jocelyn. "We yet have unfinished business."

It was going to happen now, thought Dumarest. The talk and preliminaries were over. Soon the guards would come, the crewmen and Ilgash, the bodyguard who had brought him the invitation to the meal. It had been out of curiosity, Dumarest suspected. It seemed to be something new to relieve the monotony of bored and jaded aristocrats, con-descending to eat with a traveler, but not an or-dinary man, someone who had recently killed and who might be expected to talk about what he had done. But who had, instead, insulted his host.

Dumarest tensed in his chair. Anger warmed his blood, already tender with memory. If they thought he would be easy to take, they were due for a surprise. This was Scar, not Jest. Once out of the ship, he could laugh at them all and kill them if they came for him. He could kill those who might be eager for a possible bribe. *Kill all the smug, gloating, self-satisfied fools who regarded those less fortunate than themselves as animals, beasts without feeling or emotion. Kill!*

He caught himself, trembling, wondering at his rage. *The wine? Has something been slipped into the wine? The sweetmeats?* He thought of the woman, of the thing he had seen in her eyes, the interplay he had sensed. Had she primed him with some drug to explode into a mindless fury, to kill her husband?

"Drink this," said Jocelyn. He stood beside Dumarest, a glass of foaming effervescence in his hand. "Drink," he said sharply. "You ate and drank an unusual combination; the effects can sometimes be peculiar."

Dumarest gulped the foaming liquid.

"Adrienne has a peculiar sense of the ridicu-lous," said Jocelyn conversationally. "I think she must have acquired it on her home world; Eldfane is a barbarous place. Have you been there?"

"No, my lord." Dumarest rose. "With your permission, I think I should go now."

"And, if I refuse?" Jocelyn smiled. "But why should I refuse? If you wish to leave, none will prevent you. But I should regard it as a favor if you stay." He poured two glasses full of sparkling red wine. "Here." He held them both at arms length. "Take your choice."

Their eyes met. "You are well to be cautious," said Jocelyn. "But I give you my word as the ruler of a planet that you have nothing to fear, from me, at least. I cannot speak for others."

Dumarest took one of the glasses. "From the Lady Adrienne, my lord?"

"I was thinking of the cyber," said Jocelyn. "You don't like him, do you?"

"I have reason to detest his breed."

"So we have at least one thing in common." Jocelyn sipped his wine. "Yeon is a gift, a part of Adrienne's dowry. Often I wonder as to the generosity of my father-in-law. The services of the Cyclan do not come cheap."

"There is a saying, Beware of those bearing gifts!"

"A wise adage." Jocelyn put down his empty glass. "Tell me, Earl, do you believe in destiny?"

"Fate? The belief that a thing must happen, no matter what a man does to prevent it? No."

"Luck then, surely you must believe in that."

"Yes, my lord."

"Forget titles. If you believe in luck, then why not in fate?"

"Are they the same?" Dumarest paused, looking at his host. The man was serious. "Luck is the fortuitous combination of favorable circumstances," said Dumarest slowly. "Some men have it more than others. From what I know of fate, it is evenly spread. A man has his destiny; all men have theirs. What will be will be. But if that is so, why should anyone strive? Where is the point of a man trying to better himself, to gain more comfort for his family, perhaps, or build a fortune to safeguard against bad times?"

"Let us talk of Heldar," said Jocelyn. "You blame me for what happened, but be just. It was his fate to die as he did."

"And the woman he killed?"

"That also."

Dumarest was bitter. "Justification, my lord?"

"Fact." Jocelyn took a coin from his pocket, spun it and caught it without looking. "Heldar's fate rested on sheer chance. Had his luck been good, I would have healed him. It was bad. He could not escape his fate." He added, "Because of that, both he and the woman met their destiny."

"Why?" Dumarest put aside his wine. "I do not think you are a cruel man; why play such games?"

Jocelyn turned and strode to the far side of the room; then he turned again to face his guest.

"A man must believe in something," he said. "He must have some sure guide in a world of insane confusion. Jest is such a world. There are three suns, overlapping magnetic fields, cosmic flux in a constantly changing set of variables. We are poor because we are cursed. Astrological influences are strong: men forget, women forget, children die of starvation because they are not remembered, things are left half-built, roads lead to nowhere, diseases change, no two harvests are alike, and everywhere grows a flower with a narcotic scent, nepenthe weed. Inhale the fumes and reason takes wing—madness, Earl, madness!

"Imagine if you can a world on which little can be predicted with any degree of certainty. You sow your seed and wait and forget how long you've waited so you plow and sow again—and ruin the sprouting crops. You keep records and forget what they are for, make notations and find that, today, you cannot read and go for a walk and sit and stay there for days and rise and forget that you sat at all. We live in caverns, Earl. We have to seal ourselves in a miniature world of our own devising because we cannot trust our senses unless we do. And we are poor. Poor!"

His hand smashed down on one of the tables with force enough to shatter the thin legs. Jocelyn looked down at the ruin.

"Poor," he said. "Can you imagine what that means to the ruler of a world? I married Adrienne for her dowry and for the son I hope she will give me. I came to Scar because of accident and because I must follow every chance guide, hoping that fate is leading me to prosperity. I made Jellag Haig a baron because I have nothing but titles to bestow. I need him and his knowledge. He knows his trade. Perhaps he can evolve a strain of fungi to kill the nepenthe weed. If he does, I shall make him a duke. I forced Heldar to test his luck because, on Jest, an unlucky man does not live long. I do what I must, Earl, because I have no choice. And I make a jest of life because, if I did not, I would spend my life in tears!"

Yeon paused, stepping back to allow Adrienne entrance to her cabin. She opened the door, saw the compartment was empty and gestured for the cyber to follow her inside. A drifting red shadow, he obeyed her command. Patiently he waited for her to speak.

"Have you fully assimilated the tapes on Jest, yet, Yeon?"

"There is much to be learned, my lady."

"Answer the question! Have you?"

He guessed what was on her mind. "There are no laws preventing your claiming the throne should the present ruler die." he said deliberately. "But there is a provision as to the nearest relative. If you had no issue, your right could be challenged. It would mean an inquiry as to who could provide the greatest good. As a stranger, you would have little chance of winning the majority vote of the Council."

"And if I had a child?"

"In that case, there would be no argument. The child would inherit and you would be regent."

She nodded, almost satisfied, but there was one other matter. "If I should be pregnant?"

"Again, an inquiry to determine the ancestry of the child. Tests would be made. It would be far better for the present ruler to recognize his heir. No inquiry, then, would be made." He anticipated her next question. "In the case of you having a proven heir and your husband dying, you would become regent. If you should marry again your new husband would become your consort with no actual power other than a seat on the Council."

She inhaled, expanding her chest. "So I am stuck with the fool until he fathers a child. Is that what you are saying?"

"I am advising you, my lady. I can do no more."

"A pity." But she had her answer. *First the child and then, with my position secure, a man to keep me company, a real man. Dumarest?* She smiled. Anything was possible. "Very well," she said to the cyber. "That will be all."

Quietly he left the room. His own cabin was on an upper level, a small cubicle containing little more than a cot. Carefully he locked the door and touched the wide bracelet about his left wrist. The device ensured that he would remain safe from spying eyes; no electronic scanner could focus on his vicinity. It was an added precaution, nothing more.

Lying supine, he relaxed, closing his eyes and concentrating on the Samatchazi formulae. Gradually he lost the senses of taste, touch, smell and hearing. Had he opened his eyes he would have been blind. Locked in the prison of his skull, his brain ceased to be irritated by external stimuli; it became a thing of pure intellect, its knowledge of self its only thread of individual life. Only then did the grafted Homochon elements become active. Full rapport followed.

Yeon expanded with added dimensions.

Each cyber had a different experience. For him it was as if he were a crystal multiplying in geometric progression, doubling himself with every flicker of time, the countless facets opening paths in darkness so as to let in the shining light of truth. He was a living part of an organism which stretched across space in innumerable facets each glowing with intelligence. Crystals connected one to the other in an incredibly complex mesh of lines and planes stretching to infinity. He was a part of it and all of it at the same time, the lesser merging with the greater to form a tremendous gestalt of minds.

At the heart of the multiple crystal was the head-quarters of the Cyclan. Buried beneath miles of rock, deep in the heart of a lonely planet, the central intelligence absorbed his knowledge as a sponge sucks up water. There was nothing as slow as verbal communication, just a mental communion in the form of words: quick, almost instantaneous, organic transmission against which even the multiple-light speed of supra-radio was the merest crawl.

"Verification of anticipated movement of quarry received. Obtain ring and destroy Dumarest."

There was nothing else aside from sheer, mental intoxication.

There was always a period after rapport during which the Homochon elements sank back into quiescence and the machinery of the body began to realign itself with mental control. Yeon floated in a dark nothingness while he sensed strange memories and associations, unlived situations and exotic scenes, the scraps of overflow from other intelligences, the waste of other minds. They were of the central intelligence of the tremendous cybernetic complex which was the heart of the Cyclan.

One day he too would be a part of that gigantic intelligence. His body would be discarded and his mind incorporated with others, similarly rid of hampering flesh, hooked in series, immersed in nutrient fluids and fed by ceaseless mechanisms.

There were more than a million of them, brains without number, freed intelligences, potentially immortal, working in harmony to solve all the problems of the universe. The reward for which every cyber longed was the time when he could take his place in the gestalt of minds to which there could be no imaginable resistance or end.

Chapter Seven

Dumarest looked at the instrument strapped to his left wrist, studying the needles beneath the plastic cover. One held steady on the magnetic pulse transmitted from the station, the other swung a little as it pointed to the right. He said, "To the right eight degrees. Got it?"

Clemdish bent over a map as he squatted on the ground. "That will be number four," he said, his voice muffled a little as it came through the diaphram of his suit. "The next will be on the left and then two more to the right." He rose, folding the map and slipping it into a pocket. "We're on course, Earl, and making good time."

"So far," said Dumarest. "Let's hope we can keep it up." He lifted his shoulders, easing the weight of the pack on his back, and checked the rest of his gear with automatic concern. "All right," he said. "Let's get moving."

There was an eeriness about Scar in late summer, a stillness, as if nature were preparing for something spectacular, gathing its energies before erupting into violence. The air was oppressive with heat and tension; there was no sound other than that they made as they walked through the weird forest of monstrous fungi.

It was, thought Dumarest, something like walking under water. The suits were envelopes designed to shield the wearer from harmful spores; they were sealed and fed by air forced through filters, trapping body heat until they drenched the wearer in perspiration. Absorbent packs soaked up the excess moisture, but nothing could be done about the heat.

The terrain added to the illusion. The ground was hard, uneven and crowded with delicate growths as though with coral. The towering plants cut off the light from the sun, allowing only a crimson twilight to reach their swollen boles. Fronds of red and black, yellow and puce, deathly white and sapphire blue hung from gigantic mushrooms; there were also buff extensions like the spread ribs of a ladies' fan and warted lumps looking like naked brains. Growth lived on growth and others were deep in the soil.

Through this colorful fantasy they walked, miniature men crawling among nightmare shapes.

"It's hot!" Clemdish halted, face red and streaming behind the transparency of his suit. "Earl, can't we take a break?"

Dumarest maintained his pace. "Later."

They passed their markers on the left and right, Dumarest checking their position as the detector picked up the signal from their slender rods. Once something exploded high above, an overripe cap releasing its spores and sending them in a dust-fine cloud to settle through the heavy air. Finally, when Clemdish was stumbling, his mouth wide as he gasped for air, Dumarest called a halt.

"We'll rest for a while," he said. "Find us something to eat, while I set up the tent."

Safe within the transparent sack Clemdish tore off his helmet and scratched vigorously at his scalp. "I've been wanting to do that for miles," he said gratefully. "I don't know what it is, Earl, but every time I get suited up I want to scratch. I've bathed, used skin deadeners, the lot, but I still want to scratch. Psychological?"

"Probably." Dumarest picked up a piece of the food Clemdish had gathered. He ate, chewing thoughtfully and examining the green-striped fungi. "Candystalk," he said. "Too ripe for good eating. It must be later than we thought."

Clemdish shook his head. "I don't think so. There was some deadman that was really immature." He picked up a fragment of brown and black. "Try this brownibell, it's real good."

It was good to the taste but low in protein and almost devoid of vitamins. The fungi had bulk and flavor but little else. It could be collected and dried for food and fuel, but those who ate nothing else quickly showed signs of degeneration. Those who deliberately selected the caps containing hallucinogens died even sooner, from starvation, parasitical spores, even simple drowning during the winter rains.

Dumarest leaned back, feeling the hot stickiness of his body against the confining walls of the tent. Clemdish had fallen asleep, his flat-nosed face red and sweating and his mouth open to emit a gurgling snore. Dumarest leaned over and placed his hand over the open mouth. The small man grunted, rolled over and settled down in silence.

Thoughtfully Dumarest studied his map.

The sites where they had left the markers were dotted in red, their path was a thin line of black. The place where he had found the golden spore was deliberately unmarked. The detectors were supposed to be foolproof, each instrument able only to pick up a matching signal, but it was wise to take no chances. At harvest time Scar lived up to the savagery of its name.

Putting away the map Dumarest took a sip of brackish water and tried to relax. Sleep was a long time coming. It was too hot and too stuffy, despite the mechanism humming as it circulated clean, filtered air. The ruby twilight was too reminiscent of the interior of an oven. It pressed around the tent giving rise to a claustrophobic irritation.

Finally he drifted into an uneasy doze in which a laughing jester danced around him with a jingle of bells on cap and shoes. The wand in his hand bore an inflated bladder and he kept thrusting it toward Dumarest's face. Then, suddenly the wand was the glinting metal of a knife and the jester wore the face of Heldar. He snarled and opened his mouth to spit a gush of blood.

To one side a figure cloaked in flaming scarlet watched with burning eyes.

Dumarest jerked awake, sweating, heat prickling his skin. A red glare stabbed into his eyes. From one side the sun shone with baleful fury, the unmasked disk huge as it spread across the sky. Against it drifted a black shape and noise came from men working beneath.

Clemdish rolled, muttered, and was suddenly awake. "Earl! The sun! The sun! What's happening?"

"Harvesters," said Dumarest.

As he watched, another towering growth fell with a soggy crash and exposed more of the naked sky. Men grappled with it, hooking lines to the cap and cutting it free so that others could draw it up to the loading well of the raft. As it lifted, sweating, unsuited figures flung themselves at another fungus, their machetes flashing as they hacked at the base.

"Zopolis's men," said Clemdish. "The crazy fools"

They were pieceworkers, risking infection for the sake of easier movement, paid by the load and racing against time to make a stake for the winter.

"Look at them," said Clemdish. "What's to stop them jumping a marker if they find one? They could strip the site and who would be the wiser?"

No one would; but harvesting took time, the teams were large and it would have to be a concerted effort. Dumarest shrugged.

"We'll stay here until they've gone," he decided. "There's no point in arousing their curiosity. What they don't know, they can't talk about. We'll eat and rest while we've got the chance." He looked at Clemdish. "If the harvesters have got this far the rest won't be far behind," he reminded. "Some of them could be looking for us."

"The rope," said Clemdish. "Don't rub it in."

"I wasn't, but we've got to move fast and get to the hills before anyone else. Once we start to climb we'll be at a disadvantage." He smiled at the serious face close to his own. "So you'd better get your scratching done while you've the chance. Once we start moving I don't want to stop."

"Not even for sleep, Earl?"

"No," said Dumarest, remembering his dream.

"Not even for sleep."

The hills had changed. Now, instead of a scarred and crevassed slope leading up to jagged peaks, a colorful mass of disguising fungi stretched in disarray. There was no possibility of standing back, selecting a route and checking to see alternatives and difficulties. They would have to climb it the hard way, testing every inch and praying they would meet no serious obstacles.

Dumarest flexed his arms. His shoulders ached from the weight of the pack and the necessity of cutting a path. He turned, looking back the way they had come. They had left a trail but how obvious he could only guess.

A growth fell and opened a wider window towards the hills. Clemdish called from where he stood with his machete, "That enough, Earl?"

"That should do it. Find some stones now so we can make a couple of mallets."

Despite their size, the growths were weak. With care it was possible to climb one, but only if it was the right kind and buttressed by others. As Clemdish moved off, questing like a dog for the required stones, Dumarest chopped a series of steps in a warted bole and eased himself upwards.

Halfway up he paused. The tiny clearing they had made gave him a fair field of view. Carefully he studied the slope ahead.

The ground itself was impossible to see but the fungi provided a guide; some grew thicker and taller than others of the same type. *Stony ground? Bared rock inhibiting the smaller growth's development?* Water would have been trapped in shallow basins, cups scooped by the action of rain and probably ringed with rock. Such places would provide fertile ground for moisture-hungry rootlets. Certain of the molds and slimes preferred a smooth surface on which to spread. Exposed boulders would provide such conditions.

Clemdish looked up as Dumarest climbed down from his vantage point. He was crouched over a couple of rocks, lashing a cradle about each so that they could be carried slung over a wrist. Each stone weighed about ten pounds.

"The best I could find," he said, handing one to Dumarest. "But they should do the job. Do we share the stakes?"

"Stakes and rope, both," said Dumarest. The stakes were rods of metal two feet long; the rope was of synthetic fiber, thin but strong. He took a deep breath, conscious of his fatigue, the sticky interior of the suit and the soreness of his sweat-softened skin. They had slept on reaching the hills, but the rest hadn't done much good. "All right," he said. "Let's get at it."

The first part wasn't too bad. The lower slope was gentle and it was merely a matter of walking uphill; then, as the gradient became more pronounced, the fungi itself acted as a ladder. Clemdish lunged ahead, fatigue ignored now that he was so near a fortune. He clawed his way around swollen boles, kicking free masses of fragile growth as he dug the toes of his boots into the spongy material. For a while he made good progress then, abruptly, he came to a halt.

"I can't get a purchase up here, Earl." Slime coated his gloves and glistened on his suit and boots. "This damn mold's all over the place."

Dumarest frowned, remembering. "Try moving

to your left," he said. "About ten yards should do it."

Clemdish grunted and obeyed. Again he forged upwards, his boots sending little showers of dust and fungi down at his partner, the showers ceasing as he came to a halt again.

Dumarest looked up at an overhang.

"We'll use a stake," he decided. "Slam one in to your right. I'll anchor a rope and try to climb higher. If I make it, you can knock the stake free and use the rope to join me."

It was elementary mountaineering made difficult because they couldn't see what lay ahead. It was doubly difficult because the crushed fungi coated the ground with slippery wetness. Dumarest clawed his way upward, his fingers hooking before he dared to shift the weight from his feet and his toes searching for a hold before he could move his hands.

With a final effort, he dragged himself onto a narrow ledge. A boulder showed at the base of a fungus. He reached it and, using the rock dangling from his wrist, hammered a stake into the ground. Hitching the rope around it, he tugged and waited for Clemdish to join him.

"Made it," said the little man as he caught his breath. "No trouble at all, Earl. I'll tackle the next one."

Slowly they moved upward. Once Clemdish slipped and fell to hang spinning on the end of the rope. Dumarest hauled him up, changed places and tried the climb himself. His extra height gave him an advantage, and he managed to find a shallow gully running up and to one side. It led to a boulder, to a hidden crevasse into which they almost fell, to a gully filled with a spongy mass of slimy growth through which they clawed, and up to an almost clear area from which they could see back over the plain.

Dumarest sprawled on the shadowed ground. "We'll rest," he said. "Cool down, and replace our filters while we're at it." He looked sharply at Clemdish. "Are you all right?"

"I'm beat." Clemdish scraped a mass of crushed fungi from his suit's diaphragm. "This is knocking the hell out of me," he admitted. "We ought to get out of these suits, Earl, sleep, maybe. Have something to eat at least. Much more of this, and we won't be much good when we hit the top."

Clemdish made sense. Dumarest leaned back, conscious of the quiver of overstrained muscles, the jerk of overtired nerves and knowing that he had driven them both too hard. The worst part of the journey was still before them; the steep, treacherous slope on the far side of the hills and the cliff falling to the sea. Tired men could easily make mistakes and one could be fatal.

"All right," he said. "We'll set up the tent, check the suits and have something to eat."

"Something good," said Clemdish, reviving a little. "I've got a can of meat in the pack."

It was good meat. They followed it with a cup of basic, spacemen's rations, a creamy liquid thick with protein, laced with vitamins and sickly with glucose. Moving awkwardly in the limited confines of the tent, Clemdish stripped and laved his body with a numbing compound to kill the irritation of sensitive skin.

As he worked, Dumarest looked back over the plain. The sun was swinging down to the far horizon, past its zenith now, but still with a quarter of the way to go. Already he thought he could see a tinge of growing cloud on the skyline. He thought it his imagination, probably, for when the rain clouds gathered, they came rolling from the sea to hang in crimson menace before shedding their tons of water.

In the distance, he could see the tiny motes of rafts as harvesters gathered their crop. As he watched, one seemed to grow, almost swelling as it rode high above the plain.

"It's coming towards us." Clemdish finished wriggling back into his clothes and suit to be fully protected aside from his helmet. "What's it doing this far out from the station?"

"Scouting, probably." Dumarest frowned as the raft came steadily closer. They were a long way from the harvesting sheds, and scouts worked in a circle rather than a straight line. Distance equaled money when it came to collecting the crop, and never before, to his knowledge, had they ever harvested close to the hills.

Clemdish scowled at the nearing vehicle. "It's a scout, right enough," he admitted. "One of Zopolis's machines. But who the hell ever heard of a scout carrying three men?" He looked at his partner. "Are they looking for us, Earl? Is that what you think?"

"They could be."

"That rope." Clemdish bit his lower lip. "I must have been crazy, Earl. I'm sorry."

Dumarest didn't answer. It was too late for regret. If the men in the raft were searching for them, they would either find them or not. Nothing else really mattered.

He watched as the raft came closer, then veered along the line of the hills, the men inside using binoculars to examine the terrain. It rose, circled and returned, dropping towards the plain as if those inside had seen something of interest.

Clemdish sighed as it turned and went back the way it had come. "They didn't see us, Earl," he said. "They didn't find what they were looking for."

Dumarest wasn't sure.

Wandara glowered at the pilot of the raft. "Come on!" he yelled. "What you waiting for?"

The man scowled but lowered the vehicle carefully to the weighing plate of the scale. He cut the anti-gravs and sat, waiting.

The overseer checked the weight, made a notation on his clipboard and climbed up to the open control bench. Behind a low seat, the loading well of the raft was open to the sky. He looked at the mass of fungi, then glared at the pilot.

"You're cutting too far down the stalk," he said. "We want the caps and don't you forget it. Return with a load like this again, and I'll knock it off your pay. Understand?"

"Why tell me?" The man was overtired, jumpy and quick to take offense. "I just drive this thing."

"That's why I'm telling you," snapped Wandara. "You tell the others. Now get unloaded and remember what I said."

He jumped down as the raft lifted and rose above a hopper. The under-flaps opened and the mass of fungi fell into the chute. Two men with poles rammed it down as the raft drifted away, under-flaps closing as it went.

Zopolis came out of the processing shed, a blast of cold air followed him into the sunshine. He looked at the raft and then at the overseer. "I heard you shouting. Anything wrong?"

"Nothing I can't handle, Boss."

"They trying to load us up with stalk instead of caps?"

"The usual, Boss. Nothing to worry about. They're just getting a little tired."

Tired and greedy, thought Zopolis, *but that's to be expected.* The five-percent cut hadn't been popular and the men were probably trying to get their own back by careless work. Up to a point it could be tolerated, but beyond that he'd have to clamp down.

"How's the new man, the one on the scout," he said.

Wandara didn't look at the agent. "No complaints as yet, Boss."

"I hope there won't be any," said Zopolis. "I didn't like putting a brand-new worker on a job like that. You sure he knows what it's all about?"

"I checked him out good." Wandara was sullen. "Tested him on twenty-three types, and he could name them all; knows about harvesting, too. He did the same kind of work on Jamish."

Zopolis frowned. "That's an aquatic world."

"That's right, Boss," agreed Wandara. "He was scouting for fish and weed. Underwater work, but the same in principle: hunt and find, find and report, report and lead. Only here he doesn't have to lead, just send in the coordinates."

"As long as he does that," said Zopolis. "I don't want the men to be idle. They won't like losing pay, and the company won't like losing produce." He dabbed at his sweating face. "How are we on bulk?"

"On schedule, Boss."

"Let me see your board." Zopolis took it and pursed his lips as he read the figures. "We're running too high on candystalk. Better cut down and concentrate on bellapellara. Get that scout of yours to locate it for us." He looked up as the raft came drifting towards the weighing plate. "What the hell's happened there?"

A man sat slumped beside the pilot. He whimpered as the overseer jumped up beside him. A tourniquet was bound about his left arm above the stump of his wrist. His left hand had been neatly severed.

"What is it?" demanded Zopolis. "What's wrong with him."

"Hand gone, Boss." Wandara looked at the pilot. "Quarrel?"

"Accident. They were chopping a bole and someone took one cut too many. That or he didn't move fast enough. Do we get another helper?"

"You just wait a while." Wandara helped down the injured man, his face shining with sweat and exertion. "Take it easy, man, you'll be all right," he soothed. "You got insurance?"

"That's a joke."

"Any money at all?" With money he could buy a new hand, but who in Lowtown had money? "Any friends? Someone to look after you?"

"Just fix my hand," said the man. His eyes were dilated and he was still in shock. "Just fix me up and let me get back to work."

"Sure," soothed Wandara. "Next year, maybe. Now this is what you do: go and find the monks, tell Brother Glee that I said to fix that stump." He looked at Zopolis. "That right, Boss?"

Zopolis shrugged. "Why not? It's the best thing he can do. Better pay him off so he'll have something to buy drugs with. Count in this load." Then, to the pilot of the raft, he said, "Well, what are you waiting for?"

"Weigh me in," snapped the man, "and forget that other helper. We'll split between those that are left. Hurry," he shouted as Wandara watched the injured man walk away towards the portable church. "We've got a living to earn."

It's started, thought Wandara as he checked the load and gave the man the signal to go ahead. *A lopped-off hand and who could tell if it's an accident or not?* Most probably it was, but who was really to blame, the man who had swung the machete, the man who had left his hand in the way, or the man who had cut the rate and so made them work all the harder?

It's all right for Zopolis. He can linger in the processing sheds where it's nice and cold and he doesn't have to check each load, sweating in the sun, driving men to the limit of their tolerance. There would be fights before the harvest was over, more men with "accidental" wounds, others who would come back screaming with the pain of searing acid or not come back at all with parasitical spores taking root in skin and lungs. They should wear their suits at all times, but how could they work like dogs dressed like that? So they took a chance and some of them paid for it.

Too many paid for it.

They paid for the greed of a company that didn't

give a damn what happened as long as they made their profits.

"Don't forget what I said about that new scout you took on," said Zopolis. "Keep him at it."

"I'll do that," said Wandara. "Leave it to me, Boss."

Leave it all to me, he thought as the agent vanished into the cold interior of the processing shed. *The hiring, the firing, the lot. But don't ask me to get rid of the new man, not when he paid me more than his wages to get the job.*

In this life, a man's a fool not to look after himself.

Chapter Eight

The crimson shadows made it difficult to see and the sweat running into his eyes made it almost impossible. Dumarest blinked, wishing that he could remove his helmet, wipe his face and feel the soft wind from the sea. He blinked again, squinting at the stake held in his left hand. The cradled rock in his right hand seemed to weigh a ton. Slowly he lifted it and swung it against the head of the stake.

He did it slowly, because he ached with fatigue, because it was important he hit the target, and because he clung precariously to the slope and any sudden shift would send him from his hold.

If the upper stake didn't hold, both he and Clemdish would fall down to the cliff and the waiting sea.

Again he swung the crude mallet, feeling the jolt through both wrists as the dulled point bit deeper into the sun-baked dirt. When the stake was fifteen inches deep, he looped the rope around in a clove hitch.

"All right, start moving," he called to Clemdish.

Like a spider, the little man eased himself from where he sprawled against the almost sheer surface. The sound of his rock as he knocked free his stake

122

was swallowed by the surrounding fungi, which made the descent even more perilous. Dumarest caught Clemdish by the foot as he scrabbled closer and guided it to the safety of the stake. He could hear the sound of the small man's breathing, harsh and ragged as it came through the diaphram of his suit.

"Are you all right?"

"I'll manage," said Clemdish. He had no choice, but the pretense gave him comfort. "We're too close to go back now."

"Rest a minute," advised Dumarest. "Catch your breath and study what you're going to do next."

Move over and down to the right, he thought. *Find a spot where you can halt and slam in a stake. Loop the rope around it while I follow and pass and repeat what we've done before. How often?* He'd lost count. But the clump of golden spore couldn't be far now, not if the detector was correct, and there was no reason to think it was not. It was just a matter of moving like flies over the cluttered slope until they reached the haven of their destination.

Elementary mountaineering.

They had lost too many stakes; the four they had left were dull. They were both tired, too tired for safety, almost too tired to continue. But there was nothing else they could do.

Dirt and broken scraps of fungi showered as Clemdish scrabbled across the slope and downward, to where the golden spore should be. He halted and Dumarest heard the slow hammering of his rock, the silence and the call.

"All right, Earl."

The stake was stubborn and hard to shift.

Dumarest left it knotted to the rope as he moved towards the little man; that way there was no danger of it slipping from his belt. He reached his partner, rested for a moment, and checked his position. The next leg would have to be almost straight down. Once he slipped and fell five feet before managing to roll into a clump of fungus. It yielded, but not before he had found new holds. He felt a tug at his waist and called for more slack. As he began to hammer in a stake, Clemdish fell.

He dropped the length of his rope and swung, hands and feet busy as they sought new holds. Before he could find them, the stake tore free.

Dumarest heard a yell and saw a shower of dirt and the plummeting figure of the little man. Fifty feet of rope separated them. When Clemdish reached the end of the slack, he would be torn from his holds. The stake was barely an inch deep, it would never support their combined weight.

Dumarest tore it free and flung himself to one side.

It was a gamble. Lower down and a little to his right, he'd seen a mound of slime which could have covered a boulder. If it did and he could get the other side of it so that the rope would hit the barrier, it could save both their lives.

He hit, rolling through yielding fungi and clawing as he rolled to gain more distance. He felt a savage jerk at his waist and then something slammed with great force against his back, almost stunning him with the impact. He managed to turn his head and saw naked rock where the rope had scraped it free of slime. The rope itself was pressed hard against the lower edge, taut as it pulled at his waist.

At the other end of it Clemdish would be suspended.

Dumarest laid his hand on the rope and felt vibration as if Clemdish were swinging or spinning. He waited until it had died and then, lifting his feet, managed to get his boots against the boulder. Gently he pressed, throwing himself back so as to gain purchase on the rope, sweating for fear the boulder would suddenly rip free from its bed.

The rock held. Legs straightened, Dumarest began to haul up the rope. It was a direct pull with all the disadvantages of an awkward position. Sweat ran into his eyes as he hauled hand over hand, the muscles in back and shoulders cracking with the strain. Twice he had to pause and rest. Once he shifted position as he imagined he felt the boulder move a little beneath his feet. Finally, a suited figure appeared on the other side of the stone.

"Help me!" snapped Dumarest. "Take your weight. Quickly! If this boulder goes, we're both dead."

Clemdish lifted his hands and clawed at the dirt and the stone. Dumarest snagged the slack of the rope around his shoulders and, reaching back, managed to hammer in a stake. Looping the rope around it, he relaxed a little. Now, even if the boulder should fall, they still had a chance.

"All right," he said. "Up you come."

Lowering himself, he caught Clemdish by the shoulders and heaved.

"Earl!"

"Come on!" snapped Dumarest. "Use your feet, man. Get over this edge."

"I can't, Earl." Clemdish scrabbled with both

hands, found a purchase and tugged as Dumarest
heaved. Together they fell back against the support
of the boulder. Clemdish sagged, his breathing
loud and broken, and Dumarest took up more of
the slack.

For the first time he looked behind him.

A clump of twisted candysticks, striped in an
elaborate pattern of red and black and topped with
pointed minarets reared towards the crimson sky.
Golden spore!

"Look," said Dumarest. "We've found it. We're
at the jackpot!"

Clemdish stirred sluggishly, his hands moving as
if trying to raise his chest. Dumarest frowned and
stared at the face beyond the transparency. It was
flushed, streaming with perspiration, the mouth
ringed with blood.

"Earl!" Clemdish opened his eyes. "I'm hurt,"
he said. "When I fell, I swung against a rock or
something. My lungs hurt and I can't move my
legs. Earl! I can't move my legs!"

Brother Glee closed the door of the church and
slowly turned away. Hightown was comfortable
despite the external heat and the church well ap-
pointed despite its small size. He regretted having
to leave it. Sternly he repressed the emotion. Summer was almost over and already most of the tourists had gone. All that now remained were the
hunters and traders, the professional entertainers,
the harpies and entrepreneurs and, of course, the
stranded and desperate, the poor that were always
a part of the scheme of things.

Sighing, he made his way to the exit, acknowl-
edging the salute of the guards and pausing as he
emerged into the heat. The landing field looked

emptier than it had, the station more wild than it was. Dust drifted from beneath his sandals as he resumed his progress. From all about came the thin, monotonous whine of the blowers as they created their barrier against drifting spores.

"Locking up, Brother?" Del Meoud fell into step at his side. "I wish it were possible to allow you to use the church in Hightown during the winter, but it cannot be. The maintenance, you understand— to open a part I would have to open all."

The monk smiled in the shadow of his cowl. The factor seemed eager to please. "Do not disturb yourself, brother; I fully understand. The portable church will suffice."

"You could take advantage of my offer: a shelter for use as your church and food from the canteen."

"The church will return to where it is needed," said the monk evenly. "But I thank you, brother, for your concern."

Thoughtfully, he watched as the factor nodded and strode away. Del Meoud seemed tense and more on edge than normal, almost as if he had something on his mind or on his conscience and, by offering his help, hoping to make friends or amends.

Interestedly he looked ahead to where Adrienne sauntered with the tall grim figure of Ilgash, Jocelyn's bodyguard, a step behind. The woman seemed to be waiting for someone. With wry surprise, he realized that the person was himself.

"Brother," she said as he drew near, "may I talk to you?"

He looked at her for a moment before answering, his eyes studying her face. "Is something troubling you, sister?"

Irritably she shook her head. "No—yes—I don't

know. Are you busy? Could we talk?"

"If you wish to unburden yourself, sister," said the monk evenly, "the church is at your disposal." He caught her hesitation. "I am on my way to Lowtown. If you would care to accompany me, we could talk as we go."

Adrienne nodded, her long legs easily matching the other's stride. "The summer is almost over," she said abruptly. "Shouldn't all those who hunt spores be back by now?"

"No, sister. Some of them make long journeys and many spores are unavailable until the very end of summer." It was his turn to hesitate. "Did you have someone special in mind?"

"Dumarest," she said curtly. "My husband invited him to share a meal with us. I have not seen him since. Do you know the man?"

"Yes, sister, but he could be one of those of whom I spoke." He sensed her desire to hear more and her bafflement at not knowing how to phrase her questions without betraying her interest. Skillfully, he changed the subject. "Your husband has done much to alleviate the distress of those living in Lowtown. The services of his physician alone are most welcome. And he has agreed to give passage to several wishing to travel to Jest."

"As workers, as indentured servants," she snapped.

"Until they repay the cost of passage," the monk corrected gently. "Even so, the offer is a generous one."

"The act of a fool," she said, suddenly angry. "I assume that he wants each one to spin a coin so as to decide his fate?"

"Not quite, sister. I have been given the task of

arranging a lottery. Available space is limited," he explained. "Only a few can be accommodated. Your vessel does not have facilities for low passage, and quick-time does not come cheap." He was surprised at the venom of her reaction.

"Is that why I was denied?"

"Denied?"

"Yes, I—" She broke off; her lips thinned as she fought her anger. Was this why she had been refused use of the drug which would have eliminated her boredom? Under its influence an hour passed in a second, a day in a few minutes. She assumed she had been refused it in order to save the drug for the use of stranded travelers.

"Be careful here, sister," said Brother Glee as they approached Lowtown. "The path is somewhat rough."

The houses were also rough, were hovels in which men, women, even children lived. There were numbers of wide-eyed tots in rags chewing on scraps of fungus, Their bellies were swollen and their skins showed the inevitable results of their diet.

People were working on the huts, slowly making up the walls and strengthening the roofs. Many were past repair and the materials which had gone into their construction were used to repair others. Those not engaged in building collected masses of fungi for drying and storage.

Everywhere was the smell she had once noticed in the slums of Eldfane, the stink of poverty.

"My lady," said Ilgash softly in her ear. "I do not think it wise for you to be here. These people are unused to one of your stature."

He doesn't mean exactly that, she thought with

sudden insight. *He thinks that I lower my dignity by
being here and, by association, his own.* She looked
at the children. *Dignity? Among the starving, what
was that?*

She said to Brother Glee. "The children would
require less quick-time and take up less room. We
could take more of them."

"And what of the parents? They would willingly
relinquish their children, but have we the right to
present them with such a choice? Your husband
recognized that we could not, and so the lottery.
Some will be lucky; some of the lucky ones will
yield their places to others."

He caught her inhalation of disbelief and felt her
anger.

"You doubt that? You think the poor and desperate have no higher motivation than the beast impulse to eat and stay alive? Sister, you know little
of the realities of life. You think your husband a
fool because he does what he must; I tell you he is
far from that. How often does the ruler of a world
concern himself with the welfare of those less fortunate? You are indeed to be envied, having married such a man. There are so few who, having
power, use it as it should be used, to aid and not to
destroy."

She caught a reflection of his anger, the helpless
rage born of frustration and the indifference of
many, of watching children starve while men
squandered money on things of transient pleasure,
of seeing the arrogance of the wealthy and the un-
feeling cruelty of rulers. Startled, she looked at the
monk. The church, she knew, had power and many
friends in high places. Where poverty lurked they
were to be found but, also, their plain robes

merged with the colorful garments of many a
court. She compared him with Yeon. Cybers, also,
graced the places of wealth and influence, but they
never mingled with the poor.

She shook her head, baffled by novel concepts
and a little annoyed because of them. Had she misjudged Jocelyn so badly? If the church regarded
him with such favor could he be such a fool? More
important, would they turn against her in times to
come?

"My lady, it is time you returned to the ship."
Ilgash was insistent.

"A moment." Adrienne looked at Brother Glee.
"I am a stranger to Jest," she said. "But if you have
no church there, you would be most welcome."

He acknowledged her offer with a slight inclination of his head. "You are gracious, sister, but the
matter has already been arranged. A Brother will
be accompanying you when you leave."

She was sharp. "Not yourself?"

Was his reply a rebuke? Adrienne examined the
words, the tone, and shook her head. It was a
simple statement of fact from an old and dedicated
man who did what he could with what he had, a
man who neither judged nor condemned.

Ilgash said deferentially, "My lady, with respect,
it is time to return."

Thoughtfully she walked up the path, pausing as
she crested the slope to look back, seeing the monk
now surrounded by children and thin-faced women
eager for news. The memory lingered all the way to
the ship.

A fungus exploded dully to one side, releasing a
cloud of yellow spores. They drifted in a soft wind
from the sea, the yellow tinged with red so that, for

a moment, they seemed a spray of orange blood.

"A parasite," said Clemdish. "A bad one. Get a spore on your bare skin and you're in real trouble."

Dumarest wiped the other's sweating face.

"Trouble," said Clemdish. "That's a joke. Who needs trouble when they've got me?"

"You had bad luck," said Dumarest. "It could have happened to anyone."

"I didn't listen," said the small man. "You warned me, but I wouldn't listen. I was greedy. I wanted it all. Now what have I got? A busted spine and ribs tearing my lungs to shreds." He coughed and dabbed at the fringe of blood around his mouth. "A cripple," he said bitterly, "a helpless cripple."

He lay against one side of the tent, resting on a bed of soft fungi, his almost naked body glistening with sweat. Rough bandages swathed his chest where Dumarest had set his broken ribs, but there had been nothing he could do about the broken spine.

Dumarest leaned back, his eyes closed, reliving the muscle-tearing effort of dragging the little man to a place of safety, of setting up the tent, of sterilizing them both and tending his partner's injuries. Since then it had been a matter of supplying food and water.

The water was running low.

"We've got to think of something," said Clemdish. "I'm no help like this. Hell, Earl, what can we do?"

Dumarest opened his eyes. "You know the answer to that."

"Split," said Clemdish.

It had been obvious all along. Only a raft could move the injured man and a raft could only be obtained at the station. Dumarest would have to climb the slope alone, descend the far side and make his way back in safety. Even a twisted ankle could mean death for them both.

"There's no hurry," said Dumarest. "Try to get some sleep while I gather supplies."

Outside the tent he straightened and crossed to where the clump of golden spore stood in fantastic splendor. Transparent plastic bags covered the pointed caps, the thin material hanging loose from the binding almost filled with the precious spores. Dumarest slapped each cap smartly with the palm of his hand, watching for the yield. No further spores dropped from the gills of the open caps; the harvest was complete.

Carefully he loosened the bindings, removed the bags from the caps and lashed tight the open necks. Trapped air ballooned the sacks into globes several feet across. Later he would expell the air, transfer the spores to storage containers and seal them against infection. He went to where a clump of liver-colored fronds shaded the tent, and tucked the sacks out of sight. Draping the straps of the canteens over his shoulder he began a cautious descent to the sea.

While waiting for the harvest there had been time to cut steps, drape ropes and set stakes so as to make the descent possible. He swung and dropped into shallow water. A tiny inlet showed a patch of cleared dirt where he had dug a well. Clear water covered the bottom. Dumarest hoped that it would be drinkable.

Dropping onto his stomach, he let the empty canteens fall into the liquid, bubbles of air rising from their mouths as water forced its way into the containers. Leaning farther over the edge of the pit, he sealed them while still immersed. Rising, he stood looking over the sea.

Fifty yards from where he stood something traced a thin line across the leaden waves.

In contrast to the land, there was animal life in the sea, strange aquatic beasts rarely seen and rarely caught. Out in the deep water they browsed on submarine growths and smaller species, able to survive in a medium which was proof against the ubiquitous parasitical spores dominating the land.

Protein, thought Dumarest. *Good, solid food to build strength, chemicals and drugs, minerals too, even. Endless riches waiting to be exploited but which never would be.* The initial investment would be too great. The immediate return too small, and there were so many other worlds offering just as much for far less effort, a billion worlds, perhaps. Slinging the canteens over his shoulder, Dumarest turned to the cliff and commenced the climb to the upper slope.

There he would find edible fungi and medicinal caps whose hallucinogens could offer Clemdish a means of easing his pain. He would lie in a drugged fantasy, waking to eat and drink and chew more of the caps and to sink again into a restful oblivion.

Dumarest reached the top of the cliff and eased himself over the edge. Rising, he made his way towards the tent.

He froze as he saw the raft.

Chapter Nine

It was Zopolis's scout raft and must have arrived while he was busy at the foot of the cliff getting the water. For a moment Dumarest thought that someone had missed them and had sent out a rescue party, Wandara or the agent himself, perhaps. Then he heard a cold voice and the hope died.

"You there, come forward! Slowly!"

A man stood before a clump of fungus in which he had hidden. The gun in his hand was a primitive slugthrower and he held it aimed directly at Dumarest's stomach.

"That's right," he said as Dumarest obeyed. "You're a man of sense, just stay that way. Now the machete, get rid of it." The gun jerked a little in his hand. "Careful now. Try anything stupid and you'll get a bullet right smack in the gut."

He was one of the three men Ewan had pointed out back at the station. Another sat at the controls of the raft, his face impassive behind the transparence of his suit. Dumarest did not see the third.

"Hurry!" snapped the man with the gun. "The machete. Move."

Dumarest dropped his left hand to the hilt, un-

135

sheathed it and threw it to one side. It landed point first and stood quivering in the dirt. Deliberately he let the canteens fall from his shoulder. "You're late," he said. "What kept you?"

"You're smart," said the man with the gun. "Maybe too smart. You expected us?"

"You were looking for us days ago. We saw you from the other side of the range." Dumarest looked around. Where was the third man? "We could make a deal," he suggested. "We need transport back to the station and we're willing to pay for it."

"Forget it!"

"Three high passages, honest money and no trouble. A quick profit and no complaints." Casually Dumarest added, "Where's your friend?"

"Looking for me?" The third man came from the direction of the tent. He held a knife in his hand, its point stained with blood. "No good," he said to the man with the gun. "He couldn't take it. Maybe this character can sing as well as argue?"

"Maybe." The gun jerked again. "All right, friend. Where is it? The golden spore," he snapped as Dumarest didn't answer. "You've harvested it and put it somewhere. We want it. If you don't hand it over, we'll get rough."

"Kill me and you'll never find it," said Dumarest evenly. His eyes darted from side to side, weighing his chances. The man in the raft could be temporarily ignored, as could the man with the knife. If he could find some way to down the man with the gun and get it perhaps, he might stand a chance.

The one with the knife tittered. "Who said anything about killing you?" he demanded. "We wouldn't do that. Cut you up a little, maybe, but not kill you, not right away." He gestured with the blade towards the tent. "Why don't you take a look at your friend? He might help you to make up your mind."

Dumarest felt his stomach tighten as he looked at the tent. The thin plastic was ripped to shreds. Under the ruined cover Clemdish lay, eyes open, blood ringing his mouth. His body was cut in a score of places, deep, vicious gouges above sensitive nerves, the blood making a pattern of ruby on the white skin. He was dead.

"He tried to scream," said the man with the knife casually. "But I stopped that. Cut out his tongue," he explained. "We didn't want conversation, only a straight answer to a straight question. I felt sure he'd come across when I tickled a nerve or two. That kind of pain will make a dead man get up and dance. But not him. Odd."

"He was crippled," said Dumarest, "paralyzed from the waist down. He couldn't feel what you did."

He had not felt it, but he had known of it, realizing the damage done to nerve and sinew, and not all of the cuts had been made low down. Dumarest drew air deep into his lungs, fighting for calm. This was no time to yield to blind, consuming rage; Clemdish was dead and beyond help or harm.

Slowly he walked back to where the machete stood upright in the dirt.

"So you see your position," said the man with the knife. He was enjoying himself. "You've got the spore and we need it. We've gone to a lot of expense to get it. So, if you don't want to wind up like your friend, you'll hand it over."

"Hurry it up," said the man on the raft. He had a deep, harsh voice, heavy with impatience. "I've been out too long as it is. By the time I drop you off and report in, they could be asking questions."

"Relax," said the man with the gun. "Phelan knows what he's doing."

"That's right," said Phelan. He looked thoughtfully at his knife. "Give it to him, Greck. One slug in each knee. Fire at the count of three unless he comes across."

"You want the spore, you can have it," said Dumarest quickly. "You can have anything you want. Just leave me alone."

"Sure," said Greck. "We'll leave you alone. Just deliver the spore and we'll all be happy. Now go and get it before I get impatient."

"Please," said Dumarest. "Just give me a minute. Please."

He cringed a little, putting fear into his voice, almost running as he went to collect the sacks of spore. He opened the necks of the containers as he returned.

"I'll make them easier to carry," he said. "I'll tip one into the other." He stood, manipulating the swollen bags, making two from seven, "There! Is that all right?"

Greck smiled and raised his gun. "That's fine," he said, and frowned as he realized that Dumarest was holding the sacks in such a way that they shielded his body. A bullet would pass through them without hindrance, but the valuable spores would escape through the holes. Greed overcame caution "Throw the bags to one side," he snapped. "Quickly!"

The man on the raft cleared his throat. "Hold it,

Greck. Get the ring first."

"To hell with the ring!"

"It was part of our deal. Get it, or we could be in trouble. Unless you want to run up against the big time; I don't."

Greck snarled his impatience. "Quick!" he ordered Dumarest. "Hand me that ring on your finger."

Dumarest frowned. "I'll have to take off my suit to get it."

"Then take it off. Hurry!"

Slowly Dumarest obeyed. It was awkward removing the suit while holding the sacks of spore and he was deliberately clumsy, moving as if by accident closer to where the machete stood in the dirt. Death, now, was very close. To the threat of the gun and knife was added that of the parasitical spores. At any moment a ripe fungus could fling its lethal cargo into the air. Even now a minute spore could have settled on his skin and be thrusting hungry rootlets to the moisture beneath, to explode into frantic life.

Dumarest threw aside the sacks of precious spore.

Automatically Greck followed them with his eyes, then, too late, realized his mistake. The thrown suit came hurtling through the air to settle over his gun. A shimmer of steel followed it as Dumarest snatched up the machete and flung himself after the suit. The pistol roared as he lifted the blade and roared again as he swept it down. Greck stared in horror at the stump of his arm, at the blood jetting like a fountain from the severed arteries and at his hand, still holding the gun, lying on the ground.

"Phelan!"

Dumarest cut once more; then sprang aside as Greck fell, his life gushing from his slashed throat. He threw the machete. The blade spun, glittering with crimson droplets, and buried its point in the knife-man's stomach. He staggered, tried to throw his knife, then fell face down in the dirt.

Dumarest snatched up the blade as fire burned across his shoulders.

Leaning from his seat at the controls of the raft, the third man aimed his laser again. The beam again narrowly missed, cutting across Dumarest's side, searing the plastic of his tunic, fusing the protective mesh and burning the flesh beneath. Dumarest threw the knife.

The knife plunged hilt-deep into the soft flesh of the man's throat. He reared, the laser falling from lax fingers as he reached upwards, then he toppled, falling from the seat to the ground. Relieved of his weight, the raft lifted to be caught by the wind and carried away.

A bursting cloud of spores rose from the spot where the pilot had fallen.

They were yellow, tinged with the ruby light so they looked like a spray of orange blood. The wind caught them, scattered them on a vagrant breath and towards the encampment.

Dumarest looked at them, then at his suit. It would be impossible to don it in time. To stay meant certain death from the parasitical spores. The raft was hopelessly out of reach; the tent was useless. He had perhaps three seconds in which to save himself.

Snatching up the sacks of golden spore, he raced

down the slope and flung himself from the the cliff into the sea.

He hit with a bone-bruising impact, feeling the sacks torn from his grasp; falling deep, until he managed to convert his downward motion into first horizontal and then-vertical movement. He broke the surface retching for air and weakly treading water until his starved lungs allowed him to think of other things. To one side he spotted the sacks and swam towards them. There were two of them, their necks tied so as to trap the air. He turned on his back and rested his neck on the juncture so that a sack rose to each side of his head. Their byoyancy ensured that he would not drown.

But, if drowning was now no problem, there were others. Spores could drift from the coast despite the wind and he concentrated on putting distance between himself and the land. The exertion made him conscious of his burns. Fortunately the skin was unbroken as far as he could discover and there was no choice but to suffer the pain.

He thought of stripping; then changed his mind at memory of what could lurk beneath the waves. The clothes were hampering but would protect his body against fin or scale. Thoughtfully he stared up at the sky.

It was past the end of summer. During the next few days the fungi would finish sporing and the spores would settle. To be safe he would have to remain well out to sea until the autumn and the first rains, about twelve days, he guessed. Then would come the effort of reaching land, climbing the hills and reaching the station.

It would be hard, but not impossible.

The sea would contain food of a kind and some of it should contain drinkable fluid. The sacks would allow him to sleep and the wind would prevent him losing sight of the coast. Even if he drifted lower he could still make his way back. The sun if nothing else would guide him. It was a question of timing.

Something traced a line across the waves to his left.

He heard a muffled sound through the water lapping his ears as if an oared vessel had passed close by. He turned, resting his weight on the sacks, his eyes narrowed as he searched the waves. He caught a glimpse of a line crossing ahead. It circled, came closer, and aimed itself directly at him.

Dumarest released the sacks, ducked and snatched the knife from his boot. He stared into the crimson murk. A shadow lunged towards him and he kicked himself to one side, catching a glimpse of large eyes, a fringe of tentacles and a whipping tail. The thing swept past, turned with a flash of yellow underbelly and a lash of the tail. It hit Dumarest on the chest, its barbs gouging the plastic, the impact enough to send him backwards through the water. Rising, he gulped air and looked around.

Nothing but a thin line moving towards him.

He ducked again, fighting the weight of his clothing, knife extended as he faced the direction from which he thought the creature would strike. A shadow loomed, grew huge, and became a gaping, tentacle-fringed mouth. They were splayed and lined with suckers which grasped his left arm and dragged him towards the teeth. He kicked, slashed down with the knife and kicked again as the tentacles parted. As an eye passed him he stabbed at it with his blade.

He felt the tail smash against his back and other tentacles grab his right arm. Pressure mounted as the beast dived, the wide, flat body undulating as it went towards the bottom. Desperately he changed the knife from hand to hand, slashing, stabbing, kicking as he fought to break free. Blood gushed from the creature and stung his eyes. Lungs bursting, he felt something give and swam frantically upwards. The water lightened, cleared, became air. Dumarest coughed and fought for breath. The sacks bobbed to one side and he headed towards them, throwing his left arm over the junction, letting them support his weight. If the beast grabbed him again and took him as low, he knew that he would never survive.

Around him the water suddenly boiled as something streaked from the depths. It surfaced, rising from the waves to hang momentarily against the sky, the body lacerated, the fringe of tentacles showing ragged members, one eye a gaping ruin. Then it crashed back into the water as a score of smaller fish followed it.

They were scavengers, intent on food and attracted by the scent of blood, worrying the huge beast as dogs worried a bear, darting in, attacking and weakening the creature even more.

Dumarest clung to his sacks and watched as the surface fury vanished towards the horizon. He could have been unlucky, the great beast could have been a rare oddity, but somehow he didn't think so. To be safe at all he had to hug the coast where the water was shallow, and the chance of falling victim to a parasitic spore was great.

Weakly, he began to swim to where the coast rested against the crimson sky. With care, he thought, by keeping himself wet and by staying as far away from land as he dared, he might still have a chance. He could even head back towards the encampment. At least he knew there were suits there, and equipment he could use or adapt to be useful.

He still had a chance.

There were no birds on Scar, so the black dot in the sky could only be a raft. Dumarest looked at is as it came closer. It hovered over the coast, then veered to drift to a halt directly above where he floated. Jocelyn looked down. Behind him Ilgash loomed, a protective shadow. Both were suited.

"An interesting situation, Earl," said the ruler of Jest conversationally. "How long do you think you can survive as you are?"

Dumarest studied the sky. A broad band of cloud lifted from the seaward horizon and the hills were limned with ruby light. Autumn was coming to a close, but winter was still several days away.

"Not long enough, my lord," he said frankly. His throat hurt and it pained him to talk. "Will you give me aid?"

"That depends."

"On what, my lord?"

"Many things. On your luck, for example, or on the value you place on your life." Jocelyn reached behind him and lifted a canteen. "You thirst," he said. "How much will you give me for this water?"

Dumarest licked his cracked lips.

"You hesitate, but there is no need, I am not a seller of water." Jocelyn lowered the canteen by its strap. "Take it as a gift."

His hands were bloated with immersion and the seal was tight so that it seemed an age before Dumarest could open the canteen and taste the water it contained. It was sweet and cool, better than the most expensive wine. He sipped, cautiously, fighting his inclination to gulp. Around him the water made little sucking noises as he shifted his position, the sacks bobbing as he lifted his head. He lifted the canteen again, the sleeve of his tunic falling back from his left wrist. Blood glistened from a seeping raw patch.

"A spore, my lord." Dumarest caught the question on Jocelyn's face. "I was careless. It took root and spread as I watched. Fortunately I have a knife."

"You cut away the contamination?"

"How else to stop the infection? I have no acid, no fire."

And no feeling in my body, he thought, as he sipped again at the canteen. There was no food in his stomach, but that was a minor thing. The real strain had been lack of water and lack of sleep. He had dozed, jerking awake at every fancied danger, sometimes finding they were far from imaginary. Hugging the coast there had been no more large creatures, but the smaller ones were ferocious enough, and were too agile for easy killing. He looked up at the hovering raft.

"How did you find me, my lord?"

"I have my ways," said Jocelyn. "You may thank my wife for her concern. She missed you and mentioned the matter. But enough of details. Tell me, Earl, have you been in this situation before?"

"In risk of my life?"

"Yes."

"There have been occasions when I have been close to death," said Dumarest flatly. He felt a little lightheaded as if he were conversing in a dream. If Jocelyn intended to rescue him, why didn't he get on with it? If not why did he remain?

"This is novel to me," said the ruler of Jest. "A perfect example of the workings of fate. You are here through no act of mine. I owe you nothing. You admit that?"

Dumarest remained silent.

"You can hardly deny it. So I have been given a rare opportunity to learn." Jocelyn leaned a little farther over the edge of the raft. Ilgash moved as if to grab his master should he venture too far. "To learn the value a man sets on his continued existence," said Jocelyn slowly. "Wealth is relative, as I think you will agree. What will you give me if I save your life?"

"All I possess, my lord."

"Is life then so valuable?"

Dumarest coughed and looked at his hand. He washed it in the sea before answering. "Without life what is wealth? Can a dead man own possessions? I float on a fortune, my lord. It is yours if you will lift me from the sea and restore my health."

A fire burned deep in Jocelyn's eyes. "A fortune? Golden spore?"

"Yes."

"So Yeon was right," murmured Jocelyn and then he said, "What is to stop me taking it and leaving you here?"

"Try it and you get nothing." Dumarest was curt, tired of playing. "I have a knife. It is pointed at the bottom of the sacks. One puncture and the spore is lost in the sea." He coughed again.

"Hurry, my lord. Make your decision."

The raft descended. Strong arms reached out and hauled Dumarest from the water. Jocelyn himself took charge of the plastic containers. He smiled as he saw the hilt of Dumarest's knife still in his boot.

"So, Earl, you were bluffing all the time."

Dumarest coughed again, looked at the redness on his hand. "No, my lord," he said. "Desperate. A spore had settled in my lung. I would not have lived to see the winter."

Chapter Ten

There were little noises, the clink and tap of metal on metal, a liquid rushing, the soft susuration of air. Erlan made a satisfied grunt and straightened, his head haloed by an overhead light. 'Good," he said. "Completely clear of any trace of infection and the tissue has healed perfectly."

Dumarest looked up at the physician from where he lay on the couch.

"The upper part of the left lung was badly affected," continued Erlan cheerfully. "A bulbous mass of vegetable growth which had to be completely eradicated by major excision. That was a vicious spore you managed to get inside you, a quick-grower, nasty."

He stepped back and did something to the couch. The head lifted raising Dumarest upright.

"I had to remove quite a large area but managed to do it by internal surgery. There may be a little scarring but the regrowth has fully restored the lung capacity so you will have no difficulty as regards oxygen conversion. I also repaired your left eardrum which had burst, probably due to high pressure."

Dumarest looked at his arm. There was no trace

of where he had cut himself. "How long?"

"In slow-time therapy?" Erlan pursed his lips. "About forty days subjective, a day normal. Your tissues showed signs of dehydration and malnutrition so I gave you intensive intravenous feeding. You can rest assured, my friend, that you are now completely fit and free of any physical disability, both present and potential."

"Thank you," said Dumarest. "You've taken a lot of trouble."

Erlan shrugged. "Don't thank me, it was Jocelyn's order. He is waiting for you in the lower cabin. Your clothes are on that chair."

They had been refurbished and were as good as new, the soft gray of the plastic seeming to ripple as it caught the light. Once dressed, Dumarest left the medical chamber and descended a stair. Ilgash ushered him into a cabin. Inside Jocelyn sat listening to music.

It was a sweeping melody of strings and drums with a horn wailing like a lost soul in atonal accompaniment. There was a wildness about it and a hint of savagery, the taint of the primitive and barbaric splendor of ancient days.

Jocelyn sighed as it ended and switched off the player.

"Unusual, is it not? The factor allowed me to take a copy of his recording. He has quite a wide selection of melodies and shows a particularly sensitive taste. This one, I believe, originated on Zeros. Do you know the planet?"

"No, my lord."

"And yet you have traveled widely, I understand." Jocelyn shrugged. "Well, no matter. A man's path sometimes takes him in strange directions, to Scar, perhaps even to Jest."

Dumarest made no comment.

"You disagree?" Jocelyn smiled. "And yet, what choice have you? The price you paid me for saving your life was the total of your possessions. Your clothes and ring I do not claim; the rest I do. Sit and discuss the matter."

"There is nothing to discuss, my lord." Dumarest took the proffered chair. "I do not wish to accompany you to Jest."

"You intend to remain on Scar without money and with the winter almost due? How will you survive?"

Dumarest shrugged. "I can manage, my lord. It will not be the first time I have been stranded on a hostile world."

"You are stubborn," said the ruler of Jest. "It is a trait which I find admirable. Without it, you would now be surely dead."

He rose and paced the floor. At his rear the worn bindings of ancient books rested in their cases of wood and crystal. He paused, looking at them, then glanced at Dumarest.

"Are you willing to leave the matter to fate?"

"The spin of a coin, my lord? No."

"A pity," sighed Jocelyn. "How else can I persuade you?" He resumed his pacing, feet silent, head inclined a little as if about to spring. "Wait," he said. "There is something you seek, a world, Earth." His eyes were bright as he looked at Dumarest. "Terra."

Dumarest surged from his chair. "You know it?"

"The name is not strange to you?"

"No. I have heard it before, on Toy." Dumarest caught himself. "And again on Hope, my lord, in the archives of the Universal Brotherhood. Do you know where Terra lies?"

Jocelyn was honest. "No, but I have thought of your problem and perhaps I could be of help. My father was an unusual man. He loved the past; he squandered his wealth on ancient things. Traders came from all over with their wares. They even coined a name for him, the Jester, the Fool. Sometimes I think the name was apt."

Dumarest made no comment, recognizing the bitterness in the other's tone.

"He bought old books, charts, mathematical tables together with the works of those who probe into the meaning of things, philosophers. I think that they alone can teach you how to find what you seek."

Books, printed in almost indecipherable words in a medley of languages no longer current, hardly seemed the answer. Dumarest felt a sudden anger. Was Jocelyn toying with him, enjoying his private jest? How did he expect a traveler to have the knowledge or time to read who could guess how many books?

"You would need specialists," said Jocelyn as if reading his thoughts. "You would need those who have devoted their lives to the study of what has gone before, men who dream of strange possibilities alien to accepted fact, not scientists, who are limited to what they can see and feel and measure, but philosophers, who recognize no mental boundaries. For example, I can give you a clue. Not the name Terra, which you already know, and which was a fragment of a forgotten poem, but the use of navigational coordinates. We use a common zero, correct?"

"The center," said Dumarest. "Where else?"

"Let us assume something ridiculous," said Jocelyn seriously. "Let us, for the purpose of argument, assume that all mankind originated on a single world. The ancient poem I spoke of mentioned such a possibility. In that case, where would the zero of their coordinates lie?"

"On their home world," said Dumarest slowly. "As they expanded they would use that as their point of reference."

"Exactly! Now do you see how it may be possible to solve your problem? If Earth, Terra, was the home world then, somewhere, there could be a set of navigational tables which would use that planet as their zero point. Find such a set, discover a common reference with those we use at present, and you will find the coordinates of the world you seek." Jocelyn smiled. "You see, my friend, how simple it really is."

It was simple if the suggestion that Earth, at any time, had really been the originating planet of mankind, if any navigational tables existed from that time, if he could find them and if there were any common reference points.

"Yes, my lord," said Dumarest drily. "You make it sound very simple."

"Great problems usually are when looked at from the correct viewpoint," said Jocelyn. "On Jest we have many ancient books, perhaps one of them will contain the information you seek."

"Perhaps," Dumarest ignored the obvious bait. "One thing, my lord."

"Yes?"

"You knew where to find me. Will you please tell me how you knew where I would be?"

Jocelyn laughed. "Now that is simple. I asked. Why else should I keep a cyber?"

Zopolis spread his hands. "Earl, I didn't know, I swear it. Do you honestly think I would supply a raft to men like that?" The agent's face was sweating despite the coolness of the processing shed. "It was Wandara," he added, "that lousy overseer of mine. He took a bribe to hire a new scout. The louse must have picked up his friends and jumped you."

"They killed Clemdish," said Dumarest flatly. "They almost killed me."

"I know how you feel," said Zopolis quickly. "I felt the same. Do you think I want anyone coming after me with a knife? I tell you it was Wandara who supplied the raft. And I still haven't found it," he mourned. "It must be somewhere over the sea by now. More expense, more trouble."

"And Wandara?"

Zopolis shrugged. "Gone. I kicked him out when I discovered what had happened, not what happened to you," he explained. "If I had known that I'd have come after you, but when I found out about the new scout, I held back his pay and he had to travel low. Maybe he won't make it," he added. "A man like that doesn't deserve any luck at all."

"Wrong," said Dumarest. "He deserves plenty of it—all bad."

Outside the cloud had spread to cover half the sky and the lower edge of the sun rested on the horizon. In a few days it would be out of sight and cloud would cover the entire sky. Then would come winter and the rain. If he was going to remain on Scar he had better make some arrangements, but they could wait. Something else had higher priority.

Ewan pursed his lips as he manipulated his shells. "Nothing, Earl," he said. "Not a whisper. As far as I knew you had simply gone on a long trip." The shells made little rasping noises as he moved them over the table. "Clemdish?"

"Dead. Tortured."

"That's bad," Ewan lifted his head, his eyes direct. "I'm clean, Earl. I'm no paragon, but I wouldn't set a gang of jumpers on anyone. I warned you about them, remember?"

Dumarest nodded. "And you said something else, about a ring."

"Gossip, a snatch of conversation." The shells paused in the pudgy hands. "Are you saying they were after your ring?"

"As well as other things, yes."

"And you don't know why?"

"Not yet," said Dumarest grimly. "But I intend to find out."

A ship left as he stepped through the vestibule into the open air. It lifted, then seemed to vanish with a crack of displaced air. A red flash glittered as sunlight reflected from the polished hull and then it was gone. On the landing field men slowly leveled the spot where it had stood.

"Dumarest!"

He turned and saw Adrienne. She was coming from Lowtown, her maid a step behind and a monk bringing up the rear.

"My lady?"

"You have been avoiding us," she said with mock severity as she came to where he stood. "How are you now? Do you continue to be well, no bad effects from Erlan's administrations?" She checked herself, conscious of her betrayal. No one of her rank and station should reveal such concern. "I have been working with Brother Jeffrey," she explained. "He is coming with us to Jest. I've been talking to the children and others who will be accompanying us." Her eyes searched his face. "And you, will you not come also?"

"No, my lady." Dumarest softened his refusal. "I have other plans and Jest does not lie in the direction I wish to go."

"But I thought—"

"That I have no money?" He smiled. "That is true. I was not talking about leaving immediately."

"Then you could come with us for a while at least," she insisted. "What have you to lose?"

Nothing but his life. Dumarest had met such interest before, and was wary of it. To her he was novel, someone to break the monotony, a stimulating personality. She showed interest, later that interest could turn into something stronger. If he yielded and took the opportunity he would invite an assassin. If he rejected it he would earn her hatred.

Keelah sensed his embarrassment and smiled. Brother Jeffrey came smoothly to the rescue.

"Could I help you, brother? Were you looking for someone?"

"The factor," said Dumarest. "Is he in Lowtown?"

The monk shook his head. "I believe he is dining on one of the ships," he volunteered. "A farewell party thrown by a group of tourists. I am not certain, but I will inquire if you wish."

"Thank you, Brother, but there is no urgency," said Dumarest. "I will see him later."

"And us?" Adrienne rested her hand on his arm. The touch was gentle, intimate. "Will we see you again, Earl?"

His eyes were direct. "Quite possibly, my lady."

"Why the doubt?" Her hand closed on his arm, the fingers digging into his flesh. "You will eat with us," she decided. "You cannot refuse."

He glimpsed a flash of scarlet and followed it with his eyes. The color of the cyber's robe was accentuated by the crimson of the sun so that he seemed blood upon blood, a mobile shadow as he walked from the landing field to the station.

"Earl?"

Dumarest remembered the woman. "I beg your pardon, my lady, but I must beg your indulgence. If you will be so kind as to do me a service?"

Adrienne smiled. "Of course, Earl."

"Please ask your husband to meet me in the factor's office at once, my lady. It is very important."

Del Meoud wasn't at a party. Dumarest could hear the murmur of voices as he approached the door of the office, the talk abruptly ending as he opened the door. The factor looked at him from where he sat at his desk.

"What the—? Earl! Do you mind? I'm busy!"

"So am I." Dumarest closed the door and leaned back against the panel. Yeon stood against the window with his hands tucked in the wide sleeves of his robe.

"If this is business, I will leave," he said in his even monotone. "Our discussion, factor, can wait until later."

"Stay where you are, cyber." Dumarest remained leaning against the door. "My business concerns you." He heard the sound of footsteps from the passage outside and stepped from the door as it opened. Jocelyn entered.

"Dumarest." His eyes moved from the factor to the cyber. "I understood you wanted to see me on a matter of urgent importance."

"That is correct, my lord." Dumarest shut the door. He took a chair from where it stood against the wall and rested his right boot on the seat, his right hand inches from his knee. "I intend to punish the man who tried to take my life."

He heard Meoud's sharp inhalation and saw the widening of Jocelyn's eyes. Only the cyber remained unmoved.

"This is ridiculous!" Del Meoud took a handkerchief from a drawer and dabbed at his bearded lips. "Surely you don't suspect either of us for what those jumpers did, Earl?"

"I don't suspect, I know," said Dumarest grimly. "Those men didn't come after us by accident. The man who allowed them to use a raft has left Scar—fortunately for him. But those men weren't ordinary jumpers; they were primed; they knew too much." His eyes moved from face to face. "Someone told them," he said deliberately. "Someone in this room."

Jocelyn cleared his throat, conscious of the tension and of Dumarest's resolve. "You haven't any proof," he said. "I sympathize with you, Earl, but how can you be sure?"

"I thank you for your sympathy, my lord," said Dumarest tightly. "But this isn't a court of law. There is no law on Scar. I don't need proof. I would prefer not to harm the innocent but I am going to do as I say." His lips thinned as he looked from one to the other. "I was there," he added harshly. "I saw what those men did to my partner. I know what they intended doing to me. Do any of you really think that I'm going to let the man responsible get away with it? If I have to kill you all he is going to pay!"

"Earl! You can't—"

"Be quiet!" Dumarest turned from the factor and looked at Jocelyn. "I recently asked you a question, my lord. I asked how you knew where to find me. You said that you asked your cyber." He looked at the calm figure in scarlet. "How did you know?"

"My lord?"

"Answer him."

Yeon inclined his head a fraction, the ruby light from the window gleaming on his shaven skull. "It is my purpose to advise," he said evenly. "In order to do this I take what facts are available and from them, extrapolate a logical sequence. I learned that your partner had ordered rope. This obviously meant that you intended reaching the hills. When you were late in returning where else should I have suggested you were?"

"The hills are not a small range," said Dumarest. "How did you know exactly where to look?"

"Extrapolation again," said Yeon. It seemed he spoke with amused condescension. "I plotted the routes you would most probably have taken. There were three; one had a higher degree of probability than the others. As a task it was elementary."

"There, Earl, you see?" Del Meoud released his breath in a gust of relief. "No one here is to blame. In fact, you should thank the cyber for guiding the rescue. If it hadn't been for him, you would be dead by now." He found his handkerchief and dabbed again at his lips. Tossing the square of fabric back into the drawer he made as if to rise.

"Sit down!" Dumarest's voice cracked like a whip. "The cyber knew where to find me. He could not pick one spot in an entire range of hills simply because my partner ordered a rope. If you believe that, you would believe anything. He could say how to find me because he knew where I was."

"Now, wait a minute, Earl! Are you accusing the cyber?"

"No, Meoud. I'm accusing you!"

The factor lifted a hand and touched his lips. "Me? Earl, have you gone crazy? Why the hell should I send men out after you?"

"Because you're greedy; because you're fed up with this planet and you want something better. Listen," said Dumarest. "At the end of winter two men tried to kill me. They wanted something I own. This." He held up his left hand, catching the light on his ring so that it shone like freshly spilt blood. "The cyber wasn't here then, neither was the Lord of Jest. Only one man could have told them where I was; only one man could have primed those jumpers so they knew where to look. You, Meoud!"

"No, Earl, you're wrong! I swear it!"

"You can't," said Dumarest softly. "Because

there's something I haven't told you. Those three men didn't all die at the same time. One lived for a while and he talked. He was glad to talk. He told me that you had given them their orders, that you were going to handle the selling of the loot."

"Wrong," said the factor. He was sweating, his beard dripping with perspiration. He reached for the drawer, his hand scrabbling, metal shining as he lifted it from beneath the handkerchief.

Dumarest threw his knife.

It was a blur.

The factor made a strained coughing sound as he bent forward, one hand reaching for his throat and the hilt of the blade, the other releasing the laser which fell with a thud to the floor.

Jocelyn looked at the pistol, then at the factor doubled over on his desk, a red stain widening from the knife buried in his neck.

"You killed him," he said blankly. "I didn't even see you move."

"He betrayed himself," said Dumarest. "He reached for a gun in order to kill me. I didn't feel like letting him do it."

Thoughtfully Jocelyn looked at Dumarest. The man was cold, ruthless and fast. He could have thrown the knife at any one of them with equal skill. He thought of Ilgash and wondered what protection the man would be if present. None, he decided.

He watched as Dumarest tugged out the knife and wiped it on the handkerchief he took from the drawer.

"So it's over then? You've killed the man you were after."

Dumarest met his eyes. "No, my lord, it isn't yet over."

Jocelyn frowned. "I do not understand."

"I want to know why the two men who tried to kill me wanted my ring, why Meoud wanted it. I want to know more of the three men who jumped me and the person who sent you to rescue me when they didn't return."

"Adrienne? But what part could my wife have in this?"

"Not your wife, my lord," said Dumarest patiently. "But the one who set the idea in her mind, the one who told you exactly where I was to be found." He looked directly at Yeon. "Well, cyber? Are you going to tell me the answer?"

Yeon remained impassive. "I can't."

"A pity."

"A statement of fact. I do not know why anyone should want your ring."

"But you want it." Dumarest stepped a little closer to the scarlet figure. "You gave orders it was to be taken, but you don't know why, is that it? You are merely obeying instructions?"

"That is so." Yeon abruptly took his hands from within his sleeves. One of them held a fragile ball of glass. Within it trapped yellow caught the light. "Put aside the knife," he ordered. "Quickly. Obey or I will destroy you both."

It fell with a ringing sound on the desk.

Jocelyn stepped forward and halted as Dumarest caught his arm.

"Be careful, my lord. He holds a container of parasitic spores, probably mutated, a vicious weapon."

It was a safe one. Who would query such a death on a world like Scar?

Yeon stepped to the door and opened it. The panel swung inwards and he stood in the gap, the door half open, his free hand gripping the edge.

"Wait!" Dumarest extended his left hand. "My ring. Do you want it?"

"No." Yeon hesitated, then yielded to temptation, eager to enjoy the only pleasure he could experience, to tell these emotional animals how he and what he represented would achieve their aim. "Keep it," he said. "It will be a simple matter to obtain it from your body." His brooding eyes fell on Jocelyn. "And you have served your purpose. The marriage is a fact. Even if your wife is not yet pregnant, such a simple matter can be arranged. Selected sperm taken from our biological laboratories to match your physical characteristics and accelerated gestation to adjust the time element will make her the proud mother of an heir to both Jest and Eldfane."

She would be hopelessly dependent on the Cyclan to keep the secret, to maintain her in power, and to safeguard the precious child. She could wear the baubles of rule, the Cyclan would have the real power. Another firm step would have been taken towards the final domination of the habitable worlds. His reward could surely be nothing less than an early incorporation into the central intelligence.

Yeon threw down the container of spores.

Dumarest moved. He flung himself forward, warned by the subtle movement of a sleeve, a tensing of the hand resting on the edge of the panel. His hand shot out, caught the glass ball, lifted it and threw it directly into the cyber's face.

It broke with a crystalline tinkle, a cloud of yellow rising about the shaven skull. Yeon staggered back as Dumarest thrust at his chest and slammed the door.

Sweating, he listened to the noises from outside, the bumping and threshing, muffled cries and incoherent moaning.

"Gods of space!" Jocelyn stood by the window. He pointed with a trembling hand. "Look at that!"

A scarlet figure stood outside. A growing ball of yellow frothed from the open robe, two smaller ones hung at the end of each sleeve. Yeon had staggered outside unaware of direction. He could feel no pain but the multiplying fungus clogged his mouth and his nostrils, grew on the surface of his eyes, sprouted from his ears and filled his lungs. It dug into his flesh, thrusting through the pores of his skin, growing until even the scarlet of the robe was hidden.

After a while the threshing stopped and a swollen ball of yellow fungus lay quivering on the ground.

Dumarest dug his spoon into a mound of emerald jelly, tasted it and found it both astringent and smooth to the tongue. "The cyber had an accident," he said. "That is all you need to say. The Cyclan are not eager for their intrigues to come to light."

Adrienne frowned. "But what of their aid? How can we manage without their guidance?"

"As we did before, my dear." Jocelyn was sharp. "You did not hear the man. He regarded you as a beast to be put to breeding for the Cyclan's purpose. Perhaps that would not have bothered you, but once the child had been accepted, how long do you think you would have been permitted to stay alive?"

"Surely you exaggerate."

Dumarest put down his spoon. The cabin was snug and intimate with its ancient furnishings. It only needed an open fire to complete the illusion that it was part of a stronghold rather than a space vessel.

"Never underestimate the Cyclan, my lady," he said. "Their plans are subtle and rarely as innocent as they seem. They are like spiders twitching the strands of a web so as to ensnare those over whom they seek power." Casually he added. "Tell me, do you have many cybers on your home world?"

"None now," she said. "Yeon was the only one and he came with us."

"And how long had he been there, a few months, perhaps, a short while before the negotiations began for your marriage?" Dumarest smiled at Jocelyn's expression. "Yes, my lord. Even that was a plan of the Cyclan's. You see how far ahead they look?"

"But the malfunction of the vessel? How could he have known that we would go to Scar?"

"Because he wanted to go there," said Dumarest flatly. "Where the Cyclan are concerned, there is no such thing as chance. On your own admission you rule a poor world. Men are human, the Cyclan is powerful and a poor man would think twice at defying them. And so a small malfunction of the ship, a captain who mentions a peculiar circumstance. Given your preoccupation with destiny, the rest was inevitable."

Jocelyn nodded thoughtfully as he sat in his chair. "Destiny," he said. "Could not the Cyclan themselves be instruments of fate?"

"They could," admitted Dumarest. "Brother Jeffrey could answer you better than I."

He caught Adrienne's start and inwardly smiled. Give it time and the gentle power of the Universal Brotherhood would dull her ambition. Once beneath the benediction light, she would discover an unexpected happiness in being gentle, kind, considerate and thoughtful of others—and she would be conditioned against seeking the death of another.

"The ring," said Jocelyn abruptly. "I understand that you trapped the factor, that the man hadn't spoken at all, but why should he want it?"

"He didn't," said Dumarest. "The Cyclan did—does," he corrected, looking at the ruby fire on his left hand. "But he tried to collect it for them. I thought at first it might be the gambler who was responsible for sending those men after me, but Ewan was innocent. He even tried to warn me and went so far as to speak of a ring. He wouldn't have done that if he had been involved."

Adrienne was curious. "I still can't understand why they want it, Earl. Do you know why?"

"No, my lady."

But he could guess how they had conducted their search: an extrapolation of his probable journeys and a supra-radio call to certain factors in the area where they predicted he would be. Del Meoud would have been eager to please so powerful an organization and others would be also.

Jocelyn cleared his throat. "One more thing," he said. "Why did you send for me?"

"As a witness, my lord."

"A witness? On Scar where there is no law." The ruler of Jest shook his head. "You are discreet, Earl, but I can guess the reason. You suspected that I might be involved, working with the cyber in order to steal your treasure. If I had you would have killed me."

"Yes, my lord."

"At least you are honest and do not lie," said Jocelyn. "Not when it is unnecessary, and I cannot blame you. Your sojourn in the water could not have been pleasant."

Dumarest smiled at the understatement. "What have you done with the golden spore, my lord?"

"Baron Haig has taken it in his charge. He is sure that it will be possible to breed it under controlled environments on Jest. Always before expense has limited the quantity available, but with the large amount you obtained he has enough and to spare for errors." Jocelyn sighed with pleasant anticipation. "It will make us wealthy, Earl. Independent of external aid. We might even be able to end the struggles of those who seek it on Scar."

"They wouldn't thank you for it, my lord," said Dumarest.

"I suppose not," admitted Jocelyn. He looked at his guest. "We owe you much, Earl. Come with us to Jest. Agree and I will return a quarter of the value of the spore, and I will make you an earl. You will be the richest noble on the planet."

Dumarest felt the impact of Adrienne's eyes. "I am sorry, my lord. You know why I must refuse."

"To continue your quest, to hunt the bones of a legend?" Jocelyn leaned forward, his face intent. "Why not leave the decision to fate?" he suggested quietly. "You could have an earldom and a quarter of the value of the spore, a residence and a large estate, a wife, even children to bear your name. Is this not a fair exchange for a dream?"

"And you will be safe on Jest," said Adrienne. "The Cyclan will be unable to find you."

Light glittered from the metal as Jocelyn produced a coin. "Let fate decide. If the arms of Jest show uppermost you will accept all I have named and come with us."

"And if you lose, my lord?"

"The cost of ten high passages," said Jocelyn quickly, "yours before you leave this vessel. You agree?"

"Spin, my lord."

Together they watched the coin rise glittering into the air, followed it with their eyes as it fell and looked at the scarred representation of a man's head.

Adrienne caught her breath. "Earl!"

"I am sorry, my lady," said Dumarest. "It seems that fate has decided we must part."

"To wander, to drift from world to world, perhaps even to die. And you could be so comfortable and happy on Jest. Jocelyn, tell him he must not go!"

"No, I cannot do that," said Jocelyn. "The decision is made, but always he will be welcome on Jest." He looked at Dumarest. "Remember that."

He would remember; perhaps he would have reason to regret the lost chance. But he didn't think so. A man has to follow his destiny.

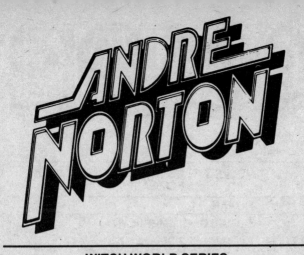

WITCH WORLD SERIES